I0780942

THE HIDDEN SCALPEL

A Park Pals Mystery
Book 1

Dwain Cassady

Copyright © 2024 by Dwain Cassady

All rights reserved. No part of this publication may be reproduced or transmitted in any form or by any means, electronic or mechanical, including photocopying, recording, or by any information storage and retrieval system, without written permission from the publisher. Requests for permission may be directed to:
dwain.cassady@DwainWrites.com.

Dwain Cassady: www.DwainWrites.com

Cover image by Getcovers.
Author photo by Becky Franks.

This is a work of fiction. All names, characters, places, and companies are purely a product of the author's imagination or are used fictitiously. Any resemblance to any actual person, place, business, or event is purely coincidental. Laurel Park and many of the locations in Gainesville and Hall County do exist but are used fictitiously. The author is not aware of any corruption in Hall County law enforcement or of any evil scientists associated with Emory University. Please enjoy the read.

ISBN: Paperback: 978-1-7361395-8-5
eBook: 978-1-7361395-9-2

THE HIDDEN SCALPEL

CHAPTER 1

He despised the sun's setting. It left him alone with nothing but the sounds of mice skittering around. The darkening house smelled of mildew. He had lost track of how many days he'd been stuck in this place. Chained to a bed with enough length to get to the bathroom, his world was now very small.

He wasn't exactly sure how he had ended up in this predicament. He thought he could remember something about being stuffed into a car. He was sure he had had a life before this. *Curse this memory problem!*

He flicked the light switch again. Nothing. *Power must be out. At least the water is working.* A pang of hunger reminded him he needed to eat. Sitting down, he felt for the nightstand and pulled open the drawer. *I can always remember where the food is. Why can't I remember why I'm here?* Pulling a granola bar out from the stash, he began to munch.

The cup is empty. I wish I had remembered to fill it before the sun went down. He stood and felt his way through the dark room, the sound of the chain loud as it dragged across the floor.

He found the sink and filled the cup. On the way back to his bed, he stepped on the chain, which threw him off balance. Water sloshed out of the cup. He took a sip, decided there was enough for the night, and continued on to the bed.

Feeling around on top of the nightstand, he retrieved the rest of the granola bar and ate it. After drinking what was left of the water, he sat and thought. *I wonder how many times I'll have to get up to pee tonight. I wonder if I'll ever get out of here.*

The last thought left him sad. *This is no way to live. Maybe I'll see if I can hang myself with the chain tomorrow.*

He slipped off his shoes, lay down, and pulled the covers over. *I forgot to undress.* He didn't bother to get up again. *I'll just go to sleep.*

A wonderful dream of fishing in a trout stream with his grandson was interrupted by a noise crashing into his ears. *The door.* Dread spread like ice in his veins.

He lay tense and still, barely breathing. Flashlights bobbed as the sound of feet came through the house.

"Wakey, wakey!" a gruff voice sounded. "You have an appointment in the morning, and we're taking you to get ready."

CHAPTER 2

A wave of sadness flowed through Ben as he surveyed the shattered windshield. A Latina woman paced, agitation in her voice as she talked on the phone. *I hope this isn't the start of a trend. This park has always been such a nice place.*

Ben Blessing, a heavy set retired computer programmer loved Laurel Park in Gainesville, Georgia. He arrived at sunrise to walk his dog every morning the weather was fit, which meant unless it was pouring rain. The park had just about everything a person could want, including a circling asphalt trail that meandered along Lake Lanier, ball fields, a splash pad, playground equipment, and a dog park.

Ben stroked his neatly cropped gray beard as he pondered the situation, his dog, Snickers, sitting quietly beside him. The sound of an approaching vehicle drew his eyes off the broken window and prompted a smile. "Hey, Fitz!" Ben called into the open window.

"What's up?" Fitz asked, his gruff voice sounding over the engine. Fitz, Joe Fitzgerald, had retired from the army and was now a former police officer.

"Someone broke into this lady's car." Ben ran his hand through his white hair.

"That's just sorry. Probably some druggie. Did you see anyone suspicious? New?"

"There was a gray sedan that seemed to be leaving in a hurry. I didn't think anything of it at the time." Ben surveyed the interior of Fitz's old Highlander, always amazed at how much stuff was in there and yet how orderly it was. "How's Buffett?"

"He's doing fine. Still singing for treats."

Hearing his name and the word treats, the large ginger cat put his front legs on Fitz's thigh and meowed. Fitz brushed his long salt and pepper beard off of the top of Buffett's head and ran a hand down the cat's back.

"I see what you mean," Ben laughed, stuffing his hands into his coat pocket against the cold February wind.

The woman was still talking a hundred miles an hour, in Spanish of course, so they waited. Fitz and Ben had become friends as their paths crossed at Laurel Park at daybreak just about every morning.

Fitz unfolded out of his car and stretched his lanky frame. "Good morning, Snickers." He bent down to pet Ben's labradoodle, generating a flurry of tail wagging and pocket sniffing. "I'm sure Zee will be here soon. He's the one with the treats."

Buffett meowed again at the sound of his favorite word and hopped out of the car to greet Snickers.

"I still find it amazing that these two have befriended each other," Fitz observed, holding the leash to Buffett's harness.

"Did you stay warm enough last night? It was quite cold," Ben asked.

"No problem. I have my old army sleeping bag. Buffett and I snuggle up in it."

"I've wondered how you manage."

Another car announced its presence with rattles and squeals as it rolled into the park.

"There's Zee now," Fitz announced, and Snickers got even more excited.

"Mornin'," the beanpole of a Black man driving the rattletrap greeted.

"Hey, Zee! You really need to get that serpentine belt replaced. It's going to leave you stranded soon," Ben encouraged.

"That's easy for you to say," Zee replied. "Money don't grow on trees in my world." He leashed up his little mutt, King, and let him out of the car, his Pomeranian-like tail wagging like crazy.

"All right, I surrender. Give me the year and engine size, and I'll bring one tomorrow. Think you can put it on?" Ben teased.

Zee, Zaderian Jameson, a retired mechanic who lived in his car, laughed. "You're a good man. What's happnin' here?"

"It looks like a break in, and we're waiting to see if we can help," Fitz explained.

Zee got out of his car and was accosted by Snickers. "Good mornin' to you, too. Yes, I brought treats." He petted the dog then produced a yummy dog biscuit. The way Snickers tucked into it, one would have thought it was a foreign delicacy. "I didn't forget you," he said, laying three cat treats on the asphalt for Buffett.

As the three men stood and gabbed, a woman who was walking along the asphalt trail that circled the park turned off and headed toward them.

She eyed the woman and then the men. "Guys, I think she's married," she teased.

"Mornin', Luna. There's always a chance," Zee grinned, and they all laughed.

"Oh, I see," Luna said, noticing the broken window.

Luna, a retired high school math teacher, had her raven hair pulled through the back of her baseball cap. At fifty-eight, she had remained trim and fit. She paused and listened to the woman.

"She's talking to her sister and is worried about what her husband will do," she explained.

"What he ought to do is come wait with her till the police get here," Fitz grumped. "What's taking them so long, anyway?"

The woman finally ended her call and eyed the group that had gathered around her car. "Sorry. I talk to mi hermana."

"Was anything stolen?" Ben asked.

"My purse. Everything but my key."

The corners of her mouth drew down, prompting concern in Ben. "Have you called the police?"

"No."

"Would you like me to? This needs to be reported. Not that they will retrieve your missing items, but still…"

The woman looked to Luna, question marks in her eyes. Luna explained in Spanish, and the woman shook her head.

"No. I no can call the police."

"Why not?" Zee asked.

The woman looked at the ground, and Ben sensed deep fear.

"She's undocumented," Luna whispered.

Ben's heart sank. *I wish people didn't have to suffer so.* "Is there any way we can help?" he asked.

"No. I go now."

The group watched as she drove away.

"Well that's sad," Fitz said.

"The wind is going to be cold coming through that window. Hey! There's Katía!" Zee said as another car approached.

The car stopped and a camera poked out the window. Katía drove on up and hopped out. "Hey, Park Pals! Just look at this picture of diversity! Two Black folks, one Latina, and two White guys."

Ben surveyed the group. *She's right. This is a great group. I'm glad we've become friends. I'm glad Katía labeled us the Park Pals, too.* "Did you get any good shots this morning?"

Katía unfolded her long legs and worked her five-feet-eleven-inch frame out of the Prius. She was a thirty-seven-year-old African American who had played basketball through college at Georgia Southern University. "The shot of the group is my favorite," she answered, looking through her morning's images. She passed the camera around.

Katía Bancroft was the only one of the park pals still employed, being the pastor of a small church. She was also an avid photographer who spent many mornings trying to capture the perfect sunrise shot over the lake.

"Y'all look so gloomy today," Katía observed.

"The woman who just drove off had her car broken into," Fitz explained. "Ben's afraid it's the end of our nice little park."

Ben looked down, suddenly self-conscious. "You have to admit, we've created a special place here. It's not everywhere in America you can gather a group of friends so easily."

"We'll just have to keep a closer watch on things," Katía said. "One bad event can't be the end."

"Watch out for a grungy-looking gray sedan. I saw one hurrying out of here this morning," Ben advised.

"The sad fact is that when a thieves have had success in a spot like this, they often come back. Especially druggies. We need to keep our eyes peeled," Fitz bemoaned.

"Park Pals on patrol," Zee quipped.

"I'd better head to the office. It's great to see everyone," Katía said.

"You should retire so you don't have to rush off," Ben chided.

"Do I look that old?" Katía retorted.

Ben sputtered, "That's not what I meant." His cheeks warmed.

Katía laughed and drove away. Ben leaned down and petted Snickers. "OK, girl, it's time for our walk."

Snickers pulled over to Zee and charmed one more treat out of him before they were off.

"I'll have that serpentine belt in the morning," Ben called over his shoulder as he led Snickers toward the trail.

CHAPTER 3

The next morning at dawn, Fitz dried his thinning, mostly gray hair as best he could with the paper from the dispenser in the park bathroom. He neatly folded and bagged the clothes he had just changed out of. Stepping out of the bathroom, he shuddered against the cold. *I hope my hair dries fast!*

Opening the liftgate, he spoke with authority, "Stay put, Buffett. You don't have your harness on." The cat obeyed, sniffing the bag of clothes that Fitz placed neatly in what he called his "laundry hamper." It was really just a spot where he stacked his dirty clothes.

"I'll be back with some water," he explained to Buffett as he closed the lift gate and headed back into the bathroom.

"Last but not least, we have to scoop your litter." He placed the water dish in its spot behind the driver's seat then went to the other side of the vehicle and scooped the litter. Dropping the bag into the trash can, he smiled as he heard Ben's car approaching.

"Good morning! I see you're hard at it already," Ben greeted.

"Hey, Ben. I just deposited Buffett's contribution from last night."

Ben laughed. "Does he really stink up the car?" Snickers wandered over to sniff Fitz.

"It's rough for a few minutes, then the litter captures it. Hey, Snickers!"

"Zee's not here yet, I see. I brought him a belt."

"That was kind of you. His car does sound bad. You'd think a mechanic would take better care of it."

"I think he drinks a bit. That might distract him."

"That's an understatement!" Fitz laughed, fastening the harness on Buffett. "I feel like a walk today. Do you want to walk with Snickers?"

Buffett meowed agreement, and they were off.

"Maybe Zee will be here when we get back," Ben said.

"We'll definitely hear him if he drives up."

"Is Buffett's first name Jimmy?"

"Nah. He's just Buffett, but he does like the man's music."

They laughed and walked on toward the one-mile trail.

"Wow! Look at that sunrise!" Ben observed as they rounded a corner and the sky fired with pinks. "God's gotten the brushes out again."

"I wonder if Katía is getting that."

Ben pointed. "Venus is still showing off."

They passed the spot where Katía usually sat with her camera, but she wasn't there.

"It's Friday. I think she tends to sleep in," Fitz pointed out. As they kept walking, Buffett pranced along, tail high in the air, like he owned the park.

"Are you sure Buffett's not a dog in disguise?" Ben asked. "He acts more like a dog than a cat."

"Nope. He's one hundred percent cat." Fitz had had his ear tuned for the sound of Zee's car the whole walk. "Still no sign of Zee. I wonder if you're a day late with that serpentine belt."

"I'm wondering that, too."

Luna popped around a curve coming in their direction. She was wearing a bright jacket that seemed a reflection of the sunrise.

"Good morning, Luna. You and the sunrise match perfectly today," Ben said.

She held her sleeve toward the eastern sky. "You're right. Is everyone doing well this morning?"

"Fine and dandy," Fitz answered. "How about you?"

"Other than worrying a bit about the lady from yesterday, I'm fine, thanks."

"Yeah. I hope her husband behaved himself. If I find out otherwise, I might have to pay him a visit," Fitz replied.

"Oh dear! Don't go getting yourself into trouble. I have to keep up my pace. I'll see you on the other side." With that, Luna pressed on down the trail.

"That looks like the gray sedan I saw yesterday," Ben observed as they came back within sight of the parking area. "And it's pulling up next to your vehicle.

"That sorry dog. No offense, Snickers." Fitz quickened his pace, making a beeline for the car. "He's not getting any of my stuff. Come on, Buffett."

A scraggly looking man with greasy hair got out of the gray car and looked around. He slid close to the passenger window and paused.

"Good morning!" Fitz barked in his police voice, and the man jumped. "It's a beautiful day. I'd hate to ruin it with someone getting hurt." He pulled his jacket aside, revealing a semi-automatic Beretta. "Don't worry. The first round is rat shot. It won't kill a man, but it does let him know I'm serious." He kept hurrying toward the man, anger building with each step.

The man's eyes got wider with each step Fitz took. He seemed paralyzed. Finally, his brain seemed to engage. He lunged into his car, banging his head on the top, and backed out.

Fitz looked back toward Ben with a big grin. "That was fun," he said, watching as Ben snapped a photo with his phone.

"I believe I'll let the police know about this guy," Ben said.

"Actually, you can't," Fitz replied.

"Why not. He's probably the one who broke into that woman's car, and I'm pretty sure he was about to do the same to yours."

Fitz rezipped his coat. "There's no victim, so there's no crime to report. The woman was undocumented, so she doesn't want any interaction with law enforcement. It could lead to her deportation, probably leaving children behind. He didn't actually do anything to my car, so the only thing we have to report here is that I threatened a man who was standing near my vehicle. I don't think the police will be impressed."

Fitz could see Ben's frustration. "In your world, the police are agents of help and protection. In our world, they are a threat. Life is quite multifaceted. It all depends on where one stands."

"You could have at least barked," Ben said to Snickers.

Fitz laughed. "I wonder if Buffett would have attacked had that guy laid a hand on his home."

Ben laughed. "That would be quite a sight! What is rat shot, anyway?"

"It's like a tiny shotgun shell. It's meant for killing snakes and other vermin. I keep one in the first chamber as a deterrent. If the guy keeps coming after that shot, I plan to go for the kill."

"You've thought a lot about this," Ben observed.

"Yeah, I have. I don't want to kill anyone, but I will if it's a choice between them or me."

"That makes sense. Still no sign of Zee. I hope he's OK."

CHAPTER 4

SIX WEEKS EARLIER

The room was packed in anticipation of Dr. Maxwell Herringer's presentation. Dr. Stanford Cole, a neurologist from Gainesville, Georgia, worked his way to a seat in the twelfth row. He was excited to hear Dr. Herringer's speech.

Dr. Herringer, a renowned neuroscientist from Emory University, was the keynote speaker for the medical convention in Sacramento, California. The consensus of the rumor mill was that he would be presenting a potentially groundbreaking treatment for dementia. Dr. Cole settled in with his legal pad to take notes.

At the appointed hour, the president of the convention stepped up to the microphone. "I'm sure we're all aware of Dr. Maxwell Herringer's credentials. He's considered one of the top neuroscientists in the world. His textbooks are used in medical schools all over the country, and his research continues to be published at an unprecedented rate.

"His contributions to the treatment of movement disorders are monumental. I could spend the rest of the session recounting his accomplishments, but that's not what you're here for. So without using up any more of his time, I am delighted to present to you Dr. Maxwell Herringer."

The applause was loud as Dr. Herringer walked to the microphone. He was a tall man with black hair and blue eyes. His features were soft. Soft hands, soft muscles. Everything was soft but his eyes. His eyes were intense, with wrinkles radiating out like he was always thinking too hard.

"Thank you very much," he said as the applause died down. "It is an honor to be here to share my work with you. After that generous introduction, I have a confession to make. I am behind on the research I wanted to present this morning."

The crowd laughed.

"You're a kind bunch. Nevertheless, let's explore the science of memory and our current understanding of dementia."

Dr. Cole sat back and rubbed his brown eyes as Dr. Herringer went through describing the anatomy and pathways responsible for memory, his discussion being reminiscent of medical school classes. When Herringer began listing the treatment ideas that had failed or had had only limited results, Stan's eyes began to droop closed. When Herringer finally got to his current research, Stan sat up and leaned in.

"I believe it is possible to impact the progression of dementia and possibly even reverse it if we can selectively stimulate the monosynaptic circuit. By increasing physiological activity within that circuit, the brain will be able to sustain communication with the hippocampus, allowing memories to continue to flow into consciousness.

"The reason I began my remarks with the admission that I am behind on my research is that I am not yet at liberty to announce the techniques we are using to create that intervention. My colleagues and I have not yet been able to bring the intervention to the human trials stage, but we are getting close. I plan to be back next year with a new and successful treatment for all types of dementia. Thank you very much for your time today."

Dr. Cole stood and clapped dutifully along with everyone else. *What a dud. I was expecting something big.* The disappointment gnawed at him till he decided to try catching up to Dr. Herringer backstage to see if he could finesse some real information out of him.

He worked his way through the crowd and back behind the stage in the direction Herringer had departed. He found Herringer with a phone pressed to his ear. Anger laced each word he spoke.

"It didn't work! What do you mean?" After a pause, Herringer barked, "Increase it to fifteen. We have to continue trying. I know this will work."

Stan stood back till Herringer jammed the phone into his pocket. Then he approached. "Hi, Dr. Herringer, I'm Dr. Cole from Gainesville, Georgia."

"A colleague just down the road. It's nice to meet you. Please call me Max." Congeniality had replaced the anger from a moment before.

"Thanks, Max, and please call me Stan. I'm quite interested in your work and wondered if you would be willing to share a little more about your technique privately. I promise not to breathe a word."

Stan felt that he was suddenly looking at an ice sculpture. Herringer's eyes narrowed. "No." He walked away.

I guess being a grump is a prerequisite for greatness.

CHAPTER 5

BACK AT THE PARK

Fitz stepped out of the bathroom to find Ben standing on the sidewalk, serpentine belt in hand. Gray light seeped into the world as the sun rose on a cloudy day. A chill wind seeped through Fitz's coat.

"How long have you been standing there?" Fitz grumbled. He didn't like surprises.

"Long enough. Zee's not here again."

"I noticed. I don't know what's gotten into the boy." He leaned into the back of his Highlander and draped the washcloth carefully over the back seat headrest to dry. "I have to get Buffett fresh water and scoop his litter before I can take off. Why don't you go on?" He was still trying to recover from the stress of finding Ben waiting for him.

"I'm in no hurry," Ben replied.

Fitz tried to pull himself into a more pleasant disposition as he tended to Buffett's needs. "OK, Buffett, want to go for a walk?"

Buffett meowed and stood still while Fitz put the harness on him. Buffett jumped to the ground and the foursome embarked toward the trail. Buffett sauntered under Snickers, getting their leashes tangled.

"Must you, Buffett?" Fitz grumped. He and Ben were trying to get untangled when they heard a laugh.

"I see the dance but don't hear the music."

"Morning, Luna. It's not what it looks like," Ben quipped.

Buffett went right back under Snickers, and Ben and Fitz resumed their dance.

"I'm shortening your options," Fitz said as he choked up on the leash.

"It's cold this morning," Luna observed. "Did you have to run the car last night?"

"Nah. I only run it if it's down in the teens. Buffett and I stay quite warm in the sleeping bag. Of course, the car blocks any wind, which helps."

"Still, I don't see how you do it. Living in a car would be too hard for me."

"I'm lucky. With my little pension and now Social Security, I have enough money to have a car and drive it. Most residentially challenged folks don't have that luxury."

"Since you have money, why don't you get a place to live?... Is that being too nosey?" Luna asked.

"Yes, it is." Anger flared, and Fitz started down the trail. *This day is starting off all wrong. Breathe. Breathe. It's OK. They're friends.* He heard Luna and Ben hurrying to catch up. He pulled three dark chocolate M&Ms out of his pocket and popped them into his mouth.

"I'm sorry, Fitz. I didn't mean to upset you," Luna said.

"I'm not upset. It's OK." The tone of his voice said otherwise. "I'm stressed about Zee not showing up."

"I think it's time to call the police," Ben said.

"Zee won't like that," Fitz protested. "If they find him, they might try to make him go into a shelter."

"Would that be so bad?" Luna asked.

"He can't drink in a shelter," Fitz bluntly pointed out.

"What if he's in trouble?" Ben asked, pulling out his phone. They stopped as they reached the point where the trail was closest to the lake. The gray sky turned the water gray. It wasn't a pretty day.

"The office isn't open yet," Fitz noted.

"I was going to call 911."

"It's not a 911 call. It'll be eight by the time we get back to the cars. Call then if you must."

"Don't you think we should?" Ben protested. "He could be in a coma in his car somewhere. He could have had a stroke... or been hit over the head and robbed."

"I think you're right," Luna confirmed. "Let's go ahead and report it.

Fitz's mind began to spin, imagining all the possibilities for why Zee didn't show up. By the time they got back to their vehicles, he had changed his mind. "Go ahead and call the sheriff's office. I don't like his not showing up."

Ben located the number and called. "I need to file a missing person report." He described what had happened and disconnected the call. "They're sending a deputy to take our statements."

"I need to get going. I have a hair appointment this morning," Luna said.

Buffett was straining for the car. "I know. You want to get inside where it's warmer." Fitz opened the lift gate and Buffett jumped up.

"Wait, why don't we wait in my car? You can bring Buffett."

Fitz stiffened. *I can do this. It's just sitting in his car.* He picked up Buffett and joined Ben in his Outback. "Nice car."

"Thanks. I enjoy it."

Fitz tried to keep his leg from bouncing. Being in someone else's car was stress-provoking. He wasn't sure why, but he was sure he didn't like it. He slid three dark chocolate M&Ms into his mouth. He tried to keep up the small talk with Ben. He was really antsy by the time the deputy rolled up.

Relieved, Fitz zoomed out of the car and deposited Buffett in the Highlander.

"Good morning. I got a call about a missing person. Was that from you?" Deputy Carson asked, pulling out a notebook. He was pudgy with brown hair and eyes and in his early forties.

Good guess, since we're the only ones in the park. "That was us," Fitz said, resisting the urge to point out the obvious.

"Fitz," the deputy nodded stiffly.

"Hi, I'm Ben Blessing. I'm the one who actually made the call." Ben launched into explaining that they were concerned that Zee had not shown up for the last two days.

"Deputy Ron Carson. Nice to meet you. Do you know where he lives? Could I have his address?" Ron asked, pen poised to take down the information.

"No, I don't. Zee's homeless. He lives in his car," Ben answered.

Snapping his notebook shut, Ron said, "There's nothing I can do here. Homeless folks come and go. He has probably just decided to go somewhere else where he can get more free stuff."

Fitz ground his teeth. He couldn't hold back. "Zee is not like that, and I expect you to do your job. You need to take a description of him and his car and have people on the lookout for him."

"I'm not going to waste the deputies' time on this, Fitz. I can't believe you even called it in." Ron glared at Fitz then slid into the patrol car and drove off.

Ben was typing something into his phone. Fitz stood, fists clenched, trying to rein in his anger.

"He was rude. I think I'll report him," Ben said, finishing typing Ron's name so he wouldn't forget. "He didn't seem to like you."

"We have a history," Fitz replied.

CHAPTER 6

The next morning brought a stiff wind and snow flurries. Ben pulled up as Fitz was replenishing Buffett's water.

"We're going to have to walk fast this morning," Ben suggested.

"Are you sure it's worth it?"

"They say walking is good for our health."

"Buffett said he's staying in the car. He outsmarts us."

Snickers sniffed around for a pet and maybe a treat.

"Sorry, bud. All I have is cat food and hands to pet you with. The treat master is missing."

"We need to do something. Do you know where he stays?"

"I have some ideas."

"Good. Let's get our walk in and then go look."

Fitz hesitated. *That would mean riding in Ben's car. There's no place for Snickers in mine.* "I could drive by. You might want to get home and get out of this snow."

"Nonsense. This isn't going to amount to anything. Let's go together."

Fitz looked up at the sound of a car. "I'm surprised Luna's out this morning."

"Hey, guys. Still no sign of Zee?" she asked as she gave Snickers a good back scratch.

"Nope. I'm trying to talk Fitz into driving by some of the places he stays to see if we can find him," Ben answered.

"That's a great idea," Luna said with a shiver. "I'd better get moving before I freeze!" She set off toward the trail in a brisk walk.

"I wouldn't want to try to keep up with her," Fitz noted, hoping Ben would forget the idea.

"It would get us done and ready to go look for Zee quicker. Come on."

Ben took off. Fitz tried to will his feet to move as fast as his brain was firing. *How long would it take? I could take him to the closest place. Maybe ten minutes if we went there and back. I should be able to hold it together that long… maybe… if I have Buffett in my lap, probably.*

Fitz lagged behind in silence as Ben and Luna chatted about the weather, whether the snow might accumulate, and Zee's disappearance.

"Maybe he moved into a shelter to get out of the cold," Luna suggested.

"I hadn't thought of that," Ben replied. "That makes perfect sense. What do you think, Fitz?"

"Maybe. I think he would have told us he planned to do that, but Zee does do things on the spur of the moment." *I'll let it lie with that. He couldn't drink and be in a shelter, so I doubt that's what happened.*

They continued to walk, and Fitz continued to stress. By the time they returned to the cars, an idea had bloomed that allowed him to relax. Luna continued on for another lap.

"We could cover more ground if you went by the shelters and I checked on Zee's parking places," Fitz suggested, hoping Ben would go for it.

"You're right, Fitz. We should do that. Let's exchange phone numbers so we can give each other an update."

Fitz froze, nerves zinging. He had never given out his number. He preferred to remain invisible. *It makes perfect sense. I should be able to trust Ben. If he starts bugging me, I can change phone numbers.* He took a deep breath. "OK. Give me your number and I'll text you mine."

After the exchange, Ben said, "The only shelter I know of is Good News at Noon."

"They do have a residential program, but you have to get approved to be in it. They do provide lunch and showers, so it would be worth asking if they've seen him. Salvation Army is the other option."

"That's only two spots. Why don't we go together? It will give us a chance to get to know each other better."

"I've got things I need to do after this. Text me if you find him." Fitz hopped into his car. *The guy is persistent. The most likely place to find Zee is Walmart.*

Fitz pulled into the Walmart parking lot and cruised around the outer lanes, where several homeless folks parked. Sure enough, he spotted Zee's car three lanes over. He parked in the next space. Hauling himself out of his car, he heard King, Zee's dog, barking.

The small brown mutt with a Pomeranian-style tail stood at the passenger window. Fitz tried to calm him, but it was no use. Zee wasn't there.

Fitz pulled out his phone and stared at it. *I said I would do this. I have to follow through.* He had to prop his hands on the hood to stop them from shaking as he texted Ben. He paused before he hit send. *This is my first text on this phone, and I've had it for two years. What does that say?* He hit send.

"I'm at Good News at Noon. Be there in 5 minutes," Ben replied instantly.

"That wasn't so bad," Fitz said to himself. *Walmart's a big store. Maybe we could have him paged.*

"I say we have him paged," Fitz suggested to Ben when he arrived.

"I bet that's never happened to Zee before," Ben laughed.

Waiting for Zee to answer the page, Ben asked, "So what's your history with that deputy?"

"It's a long story," Fitz evaded.

"We don't have anything else to do."

Fitz let out a huff. "If you must know, I got fired from being a deputy. Ron was the one who filed the complaint." Fitz saw Ben's hands tense. *Everyone freaks out when I tell them that.*

After an awkward pause, Ben asked, "Why did you get fired?"

"For using excessive force in an arrest." Fitz's hands tensed this time. "The guy was a child molester, and he wouldn't quit mouthing off."

"So the complaint was true?"

"Yes, it was true. It wasn't one of my prouder moments." He looked over the aisle, searching for Zee's dreadlocks to appear. He was getting antsy.

He didn't like talking about his past. He really didn't like talking much at all. Things had started out so easy with the park pals. They would mostly just greet each other. Then they began to visit a little. Then Ben had invited him and Buffett to walk the trail. And now here he sat, talking about things he never wanted to have to say again. *Life is easier on my own.*

"I don't see him yet," Ben said.

One of the things I like about Ben is he seems to know when not to push it. He can tell when I'm done talking. Fitz stood and moved so he could see down more aisles. Ben stood, too.

"I'm going to ask them to page again," Ben stated then walked to the customer service desk.

They heard the page as Ben walked back. Fitz was pacing. "Let's give him five minutes, then go looking."

"That sounds like a plan," Ben answered. "We could split up again and cover the store faster."

Fitz sat back down and checked his watch. "Have you noticed that Zee's memory has been a little wonky lately?"

"Wonky?"

"Yeah. He seems to forget stuff more than he used to."

"I don't guess I've noticed that. If it's bad enough, maybe he got lost in the store and can't find his way back to the car."

Fitz hurried to the customer service desk. "If Zee shows up, tell him that Fitz and Ben are looking for him. Tell him to wait here." He went back to Ben. "Let's search the store."

"OK. I'll go right and start in the garden section. You go left and start in the groceries. We'll meet somewhere in the middle."

Fitz rounded an aisle in men's clothing and saw Ben coming toward him. His shoulders slumped. "No sign of him?"

"Nope."

"I'm not liking this." Fitz's old police instincts were kicking in. "He wouldn't leave King in the car. We need to go get him." He set off with a limp.

"You OK?" Ben asked.

"I'm just in a hurry to check on King."

"I mean you're limping."

"Oh. It's an old ankle injury from an IED… A reminder of the good old days." *Good old days that I don't want to talk about.*

As they approached Zee's car, Fitz said, "We need something to break the window. Let me get my tire iron."

As he was fishing in the trunk he heard Ben saying, "Hey, King. It's OK. Man, it stinks in here!"

"You mean it was unlocked?"

"Yeah."

"That's not good."

CHAPTER 7

FOUR WEEKS EARLIER

He introduced himself to the receptionist at Dr. Herringer's office. "Hi, I'm Dr. Stanford Cole. I have an appointment at ten."

"I'll let him know you're here. Please have a seat."

Stan sat down in one of the expensive-looking upholstered chairs and surveyed the paintings on the wall. He was shocked when he noticed a small rebel flag in the corner of one of the bookcases.

He had just finished studying the last painting when the receptionist said, "Dr. Herringer will see you now." She got up and opened the office door. Herringer's phone rang as he walked in.

He pointed to a chair as he answered the call. "Dr. Herringer."

Stan sat and tried to look like he wasn't listening in on the call. He saw Herringer's eyes narrow.

Herringer barked, "I said fifteen not fifty, you imbecile! What's the status now?" He listened. "Isolate the subject from the others, and I'll assess the situation when I get there. We'll probably have to dispose of it."

Turning his attention to Stan, he stood and extended his hand across the desk. "Hi. Dr. Herringer. Please call me Max."

"I'm Stan Cole, a neurologist from Gainesville. We met briefly at the conference a couple of weeks ago."

"I apologize, Stan. I've had a lot on my mind lately, and there were a lot of people at the conference. What can I do for you?"

"Actually, I'm hoping I can do something for you."

"That's intriguing. Please explain."

Stan sat forward and spoke. "I feel that dementia is a frontier that needs serious exploration and am interested in your research. Since I'm just an hour up the road, I would love to help when you reach the human trial stage. I have a number of patients who I believe would be ideal candidates and would be willing to try an innovative approach." He sat back, awaiting Herringer's response.

Herringer tapped the tips of his fingers together and leaned back in his chair. "I see." He looked off out the window before responding. "I don't normally farm out any of my research. On the other hand, this could grow into a large study if things go well." He tapped his fingers some more. "It would be convenient having a colleague close by. Tell me about your practice." He turned his piercing blue eyes on Stan.

"I use your research and techniques for treating Parkinson's patients with deep brain stimulators. The approach has proved to be quite successful. That is my passion. Of course, I have the usual mix of CVA, MS, dementia, restless leg, and other assorted ailments. The dementia patients are the most frustrating for me. It's hard to tell if the medications we use actually have much of an impact. We really need a treatment that can make a significant difference."

Stan felt relieved when Herringer turned his gaze out the window. "You won't mind if I have my assistant verify what you've told me, will you? I believe I would like to have your assistance as we move forward."

"Of course. I don't mind at all."

"Great! I'll let you know when we're ready to expand." Herringer stood, signaling the meeting was over.

"Would you mind sharing the approach you're working on?" Stan tried.

Herringer's lips curled into a smile, but his eyes didn't. "Now, now, now. You'll have to be patient. I'm not ready to let the cat out of the bag just yet."

Stan shook Herringer's hand. "Thank you for meeting with me, and I look forward to working with you. I'll leave my contact information with the receptionist."

Stan left feeling a mixture of excitement and anger. *I wish he would at least give me a vague idea of his approach.*

CHAPTER 8

PRESENT DAY

Ben hooked King to his leash and let him out of the car. "Based on the smell, I don't think Zee has been here for a while. Come on, boy, let's get you some food and water." He led King to Fitz's car.

"Hey, King," Fitz said bending to pet the dog. "Where's Zee?" King looked around the parking lot then sniffed the asphalt. He turned hopeful eyes back to Fitz.

"You're mighty little to be called King," Ben teased.

Fitz pulled out Buffett's water dish. While King drank, Ben searched Zee's car for food. "You said Zee was having memory problems. Maybe he went to the store and forgot where he parked. I've heard of things like that happening. People will wander around until someone realizes they need help," Ben suggested.

"That's possible, but I don't think Zee is that bad off. Of course, if you add a little too much to drink into the equation…"

Ben set the food dish in front of King, and he started gulping before it hit the ground. "Maybe the police will believe us now." Ben pulled out his phone. "What?"

"What do you mean, 'What?'" Fitz scratched his beard.

"You didn't tell me not to call."

"Yeah, I'm more worried now. Besides, it will be the Gainesville Police that respond this time."

While Ben placed the call, Fitz led King over to some trees. King peed on four of them then found a satisfactory place to poop. *I wonder what could have happened. A homeless person would never leave everything he owned unlocked. Unless he was really drunk, maybe?* "I don't like this at all, King."

"They're sending an officer," Ben announced when they returned. "It'll be warmer if we wait in the car."

So much stress for one day. I could tell him I want to wait with Buffett. He bent and gave King a back scratch. *Or maybe I'll say I want to give King some fresh air. Sounds good.*

Straightening up, he said, "I think King needs to be out of the car for a while."

"You're right," Ben agreed. "Come on, Snickers. At least the snow has stopped." They paced the parking lot with the dogs while they waited for the officer.

"It looks like there are several homeless folks parked here," Ben observed.

"Yeah, this is one of the hangouts for folks who live in their cars. As long as they behave, the police don't run them off."

"That's nice. You know, I read about a doctor at Emory who is conducting research on a promising new treatment for dementia. Maybe we could get Zee enrolled in clinical trials. They might even pay him for his participation."

"As long as they don't mind his drinking, he might be willing to be a guinea pig. Zee won't let anything come between him and his wine."

"Looks like they're here." Ben waved at a patrol car three lanes over. They headed to where it had parked.

An officer got out and did a double-take. "Fitz," he said with disdain.

"Carl," Fitz replied. *This day just keeps getting worse.*

"Hi. Ben Blessing. I called in the missing person."

"Right. Tell me what's going on," Carl said, pulling out a notepad.

"Zee's one of our Park Pals who shows up at Laurel Park every morning. Today was the third day he didn't show, so we went looking for him. We found his car here but haven't been able to locate him. We had him paged in Walmart, but he didn't show."

"Did you check the bathroom?" Carl asked.

Fitz felt sheepish. "No."

"Did you check in Lowe's?"

"No. Carl, the car was unlocked, and if you take a whiff, you'll see the man hasn't been in it for a good while. He left his dog there." Fitz gestured toward King.

"Fitz, you know we're busy with more pressing stuff. We can't spend time trying to hunt down homeless folks just because they've changed their routine."

Fitz squelched the venomous response that almost escaped. "You could at least take a description and have officers on the lookout for him."

"Maybe the car broke down and he went to one of the tent camps."

"Carl," Fitz growled.

"OK." Carl turned to Ben. "Can you give me a description?"

"He's an African American, about six feet two with graying dreadlocks. Very thin."

"What's his name?" Carl asked.

"Wow. I don't know him by anything other than Zee."

"Zaderian Jameson," Fitz said.

"I'll have the officers briefed to look out for this person. If we find him, I'll let you know."

As Carl started to get back into his car, Fitz asked, "Won't you need our contact information if you're going to let us know?"

"Oh, yeah." Carl shot an angry look in Fitz's direction as he reversed the act of sitting and took down their information.

"Do all the cops dislike you?" Ben asked as Carl drove off.

"He used to work as a deputy. He wasn't a fan. I guess you'll have to take King. I don't have room for him."

"I will if I have to. Snickers won't mind having a buddy to play with. But I'd rather find Zee."

Fitz was frazzled with the disruption of his routine. *It's Wednesday. I should be at the library by now.* He checked his watch.

"Come on. Let's at least check Lowe's. You don't have anything more pressing to do, do you?" Ben asked.

He's right. Zee's more important than the library. Great goat's breath! "OK, let's go." He set off toward Lowe's, which was at the other end of the shopping center. "I need some M&Ms. Do you want some?" he asked as Ben caught up.

"No, thanks. Tell me more about your history with Carl. I've never known a cop with enemies on the force."

"I don't want to talk about it."

"OK. How about your history with Ron?"

"Let's just look for Zee." *He sure is nosey today.* He set off toward Lowe's with Ben in tow and armed with a handful of dark chocolate M&Ms.

Their page and systematic search for Zee turned up nothing. They checked the bathroom this time.

"Where could he be?" Ben moaned as they walked back toward their cars. "Did you notice if the keys were in the car?"

"No, I didn't think to look."

Checking the ignition, Fitz found the key there and it was in the on position. "It looks like he walked off and left the car running. I think it must have run out of gas."

"That's weird. If it was a memory lapse, he might have wandered off and forgotten to turn it off."

"If it was a robbery, they would most likely have just taken his money, and he'd still be here." Fitz pulled some more M&Ms from his pocket to calm his nerves.

CHAPTER 9

His eyes refused to open. He was dreaming that he was driving fast, trying to get away from someone or something. There were bright lights closing in behind him. He knew he needed to wake up but just couldn't.

Is that a hand on my shoulder? The sensation frightened him. *They caught me!* A voice filtered into his consciousness.

"Hey. Wake up. No more sleeping on the job." It was a harsh voice. He didn't want to wake up and see who it was, but they were insistent.

My head hurts. He reached to touch the place where it hurt, but someone pulled his hand back down.

"Leave it alone," the harsh voice barked.

OK, I'm not driving. I seem to be lying down. He opened his eyes, and a bright light was pressing down on him. He looked to his left, the side on which his head hurt. There stood a gruff-looking young man.

"It's about time you woke up."

"What happened? Did someone hit me in the head?" He wished he hadn't said that as soon as it came out of his mouth. *The man standing here probably did it.* He watched a scowl form on the man's face.

"What did you say?" the man barked.

I'd better not repeat it. What can I say? "Where am I?"

The man laughed. "You must still be doped." Then he called over his shoulder, "Hey, come listen to this guy. He's talking nonsense."

Another man with a tattoo on his forehead appeared. A new wave of fear surged. *I'd better keep my mouth shut.*

"Hey, what's your name?" the first man asked.

"I'm not telling you."

They both laughed.

Why are they laughing?

"Where do you live?"

I'm not telling you that, either. "What have you done to me?"

They bent over laughing.

I reached for the sore spot on my head. *I might be bleeding.*

"I said leave that alone. I think we need to strap this guy's hands down," the one with the forehead tattoo said.

CHAPTER 10

THE NEXT MORNING AT THE PARK

Bright pink and orange painted the horizon, announcing the sun's approach. Fitz busied himself with feeding Buffett and changing out his water.

"It was too cold to bother washing my hair this morning," he explained to Buffett. "I'm worried about Zee. What do you think could have happened to him?"

"Meow."

"I know. You miss his treats."

Ben parked three spots down. "Hey, Fitz. How are you this morning?"

"Not great. How about you?"

"I've been doing some research. There are a few encampments around town where homeless folks stay in tents. I think we should check to see if Zee is in any of those."

Fitz bent down to pet Snickers and King, trying to decide how to respond. *I don't think we'll find him. I'm sure something worse has happened.*

"I don't see how he could have found a camp if he just walked off from his car. I doubt he's there."

"What if the car broke down, and he bought a tent at Walmart?"

"He would have taken King with him."

"Oh, yeah. What are we going to do?"

"I don't know but check out this car that's driving around the parking lots." Fitz nodded across the park.

"So?"

"It looks like a street gang car. What are they doing here?" He touched the handle of his Beretta to make sure it was there and watched as the car wound along the parking lanes.

"They're looking for something. There's Katía's car. We need to get over there." Fitz took off across the park.

The gang car parked a few spaces away from Katía's car. Fitz was hustling along as fast as his sore ankle would let him. He assumed Katía would be in her favorite spot for photographing the sunrise.

As Fitz and Ben approached, a short, stocky man got out of the back seat. He looked around but didn't seem to notice the two men rushing toward him in the semidarkness.

Fitz's heart raced as he watched the man set out toward the lake. "Take a picture of the license plate and the guys if you can," he whispered to Ben.

They topped the hill at the end of the parking lot, and the man was halfway to Katía. She had her eyes on the camera.

"Good day, sir," Fitz called, still walking toward him. He had already moved the Beretta into his coat pocket and removed the safety. "It's a beautiful sunrise."

"What do you want, old geezer?" the man taunted.

"Just trying to be friendly," Fitz replied. He continued to approach slowly. "I like to speak to everyone at the park. It's kind of my thing. Hey, Katía. How are you today?"

He could see concern in Katía's eyes even through the dim light as she responded. "I was getting some great shots."

Fitz stopped about ten feet from the man and glared. He glared back.

"I don't appreciate anyone interrupting my business," he threatened.

"We should all be able to enjoy the sunrise together, don't you think?"

"We have company, Fitz," Ben stated as three other men got out of the car and approached.

"Your business wouldn't happen to be harassing this nice lady, would it?" Fitz asked.

The short man brandished a knife. "You'll be sorry if you don't walk away."

"Ah, I see. Today is your initiation. I'm not sure what you had in mind for my friend over there, but I'll kindly ask you to leave."

"You can't tell me what to do, old man," the guy said, taking a step forward. "I'll carve you up like a slaughtered pig."

Fitz laughed. "Will you, now?" He whipped out the Beretta and aimed it at the driver of the car. "Call off your little thug. If he comes any closer, you're a dead man."

The driver gave a vicious grin. "Well played, old man. Put the knife up, Boomer. Let's go." He glared at Fitz a moment then turned for the car. "I'd be watching my back if I were you."

Katía came running up. "Were they after me?"

"It looks like it," Fitz answered. "It's odd for them to be out this time of day. Usually gangs do their thing in the dead of night."

"Do you think that's what could have happened to Zee? Do you think a gang could have gotten him?" Katía put her hand to her mouth.

"Unfortunately, that's a possibility. I didn't want to say it, but his disappearance looks more like a murder or kidnapping than someone with dementia wandering off."

Silence followed. The three friends looked to the sky. Ben, sounding deflated, said, "That means we need to be checking the hospitals and funeral homes."

"I can help," Katía volunteered.

"Wait. Why did you aim your gun at the driver instead of the guy with the knife?" Ben asked.

Fitz grinned. "The driver probably had a gun. Plus, if I'm right about its being an initiation, he didn't care what happened to the other guy. Had I shot the guy with the knife, the driver would have considered him as having failed his test. Then he would have shot us for good measure. The driver did very much care what happened to himself, though."

Ben and Katía laughed. "Smart thinking," Ben noted.

"Let's get into my car so we're not so cold and divide up places to call," Katía said and headed for her car.

"Katía?" Ben called.

"Yeah?" she asked, turning back.

"Your camera?"

"Oh. I'm so flustered I forgot all about it."

Fitz's anxiety spiked again, not from the encounter with the gang but from the thought of getting into Katía's car. He pulled a few M&Ms from his pocket. They were nice and crunchy from the cold.

"Do you mind driving over to where we parked so I can put the dogs in my car?"

"No problem," Katía said. "But I don't mind if they get in mine."

"Let's walk. I need to check on Buffett, too," Fitz said, buying some time.

In order not to think about getting into Katía's car, Fitz turned his attention to pondering why a gang would be out this early. An idea dawned on him. "They weren't out early, they were still up from the night. They probably had an earlier attempt at initiating the guy go bad, so they kept hunting."

"That makes sense," Ben replied.

Katía pulled up as Ben loaded Snickers and King into his car. Fitz made a show of checking on Buffett, opening the door and scratching the cat on the head. "They want me to get into her car. Any ideas how to get out of it?" he whispered to the cat. Buffett had no response.

"Y'all hop in. The car's already warming up," Katía called.

Fitz chewed three more M&Ms, then moved to the back driver's side door. He waited for Ben before getting in.

Katía already had her phone in gear. "There are two hospitals. Where would they take the body of a homeless person if they found one?"

"It would be easiest to check with the coroner's office," Fitz stated. "They should know of any unusual deaths. Even if he just had a heart attack in the parking lot, the coroner would be involved."

"I hadn't thought of that scenario," Ben said. "That would make perfect sense. It would explain why King was still in the car. But why would it be unlocked?"

"What if he had the heart attack right after unlocking the door?" Katía added.

"This is a morbid train of thought, but at least it makes sense," Ben offered.

"So that's only three calls," Katía observed. "I'll be happy to do those."

"Thanks," Fitz said, opening the door. "You can let us know what you've found out when we come back around from making our lap." Through the mirror, he noticed the wave of fear that flowed over Katía's face.

"I'll walk with you and make the calls as we go," she said.

CHAPTER 11

Fitz felt a tap on his shoulder and looked back.

"What's his name?" Katía whispered, having already dialed the number.

"Zaderian Jameson," Fitz responded. *Why are homeless folks so anonymous? Maybe I'm the only one who finds out people's real names. I wonder if Ben knows Katía's last name. I'll have to ask someday.*

Over Katía's conversation, Fitz heard footsteps hurrying along the path behind them. Looking back, he saw Luna approaching.

"Good morning! I see you roped Katía into walking today." She joined their pace after catching up.

"Thanks for your help." Katía disconnected the call. "He's not at the hospital. They could see both facilities, so no need to call the other one. Hey, Luna. How are you?"

"Fine as sunshine! How about you?"

"To be honest, I'm a bit rattled today."

"What's wrong?"

"We had some unwelcome visitors this morning," Ben explained.

"Yeah. Fitz had to pull his gun on some gang members," Katía said. "They were after me!"

"That's terrible. That's horrifying," Luna said. "I can't believe that happened right here in our park. What did the police say?"

"Uh-oh! I was so addled I didn't even think about calling them."

"Katía! What were you thinking? Obviously, you weren't thinking! Ben and Fitz, how could you not have called the police? This is serious!" Luna whipped out her phone and dialed 911 before she finished scolding them.

"I guess we'd better take a shortcut to the cars," Ben noted.

The patrol car pulled into the lot where the park pals were standing. "Oh, no," Fitz grumbled.

"Fitz," Ron said, sliding out of the SUV. "I hope you're not wasting my time again.

"You probably would consider a gang attack a waste of your time," Fitz snapped.

"OK, you've got my attention. What are we talking about?" Ron said with a sneer.

"It's about me," Katía chimed in. "I was photographing over there by the lake." She pointed. "This gang guy was headed toward me. Fortunately, Fitz and Ben saw what was going on and intervened. The guy pulled a knife on Fitz. Fitz aimed his gun at the driver of the car, and the guy backed down. They got back into their car and left."

"I see. Are you sure it was a gang?"

"Yes," Fitz said.

"I was talking to this lady. What's your name, ma'am?"

"Katía Bancroft."

"That's Reverend Bancroft to you," Fitz added.

Ron scowled at Fitz. "Reverend Bancroft, what makes you think it was a gang?"

"The way they looked. All the tattoos. Fitz said they were gang members."

Ron shot another scowl at Fitz. "Let's not jump to any conclusions just because they have tattoos. Can you describe the perpetrators?"

"They were all White with shaved heads," Katía said.

"Any more details?"

"I can't really say. I was terrified when the guy pulled a knife. I'm afraid I didn't think to study their features."

"How about the car? License plate?"

"I think the car was orange," Katía answered.

"I got a picture of the license plate," Ben offered. "I tried to take one of the men, but it was too dark to see much."

"Great, could I see that?"

Ben handed over his phone, and Ron jotted down the tag number and car description. "You're right. I can't make out any details of the men, but if you'll forward the pictures to me, the lab folks might be able to enhance them. Is there anything else you can tell me?"

"No, I'm just grateful Fitz and Ben were close enough to save me."

"Fitz?"

"The guy going after Katía was approximately five feet seven, one hundred sixty pounds. White, shaved head, brown eyes. The driver was approximately six feet two, one hundred eighty pounds. Shaved head, blue eyes. They had rebel flag tattoos on their necks, indicating the CR gang. I believe the shorter guy was being initiated since the others stayed in the car till Ben and I arrived. I trust you could make out the car was an orange Dodge Charger low rider from the picture."

Ron finished scribbling notes from the information Fitz had rifled off. "Yes, I got the car, Fitz. We haven't had any trouble out of the Confederate Rising gang lately. Obviously, I wouldn't recommend being alone at this park until we apprehend these guys. We'll be on the lookout for them. I trust all four of you saw the knife. If not, we won't have much of a case. Of course, it's not much of a case anyway since no one got hurt."

Ben and Katía nodded. Luna said, "I didn't get here till later, so I didn't see anything."

"I see. Be careful, especially you ladies," Ron said then hopped into his car and drove off.

"I don't believe that guy," Fitz said, popping three M&Ms into his mouth. "What he was saying is that my testimony wouldn't be good enough."

"Just consider the source," Ben said. "He's not a nice human."

"Yeah. He's right about not being here alone, though. I think we should all be carrying weapons," Fitz replied.

"I don't have a gun, but my husband does," Luna said. "I need to learn how to use it."

"Why don't we coordinate with each other so we can get here at the same time?" Ben asked.

"That's a great idea. I would certainly feel safer, and I don't want to let those creeps drive me from the park," Katía answered, crossing her arms.

"If you'll give me your numbers, I'll create a group text with all of us in it," Ben offered.

Fitz pulled out three more M&Ms. "You've already got mine." *A text every morning about when to get here. Not good.* "I always arrive at six fifty. You can just write that in and know I'll be here. I don't need a text every morning."

"Don't be a grump," Ben chided. "You don't have to respond. At least you'll know when everyone else is arriving."

"OK." Fitz wasn't happy, but he didn't argue. He ate three more M&Ms.

"Now we need to get back to hunting for Zee," Ben announced. "I guess the next call is to the coroner's office." He did a quick search and made the call.

"Nope. No one by that name or description has come through their office. That's a good sign, but where in the world is he?"

"I hate to say it, but the next thing to check is the obituaries," Katía said. "Let me pull up the paper."

"While she's doing that, why don't you call the jail, Ben?" Fitz suggested.

"Well, that's good," Katía sighed. "He hasn't made the obituaries."

"Not in jail, either," Ben said. "I hate to say it, but I've run out of ideas."

CHAPTER 12

Fitz spent the morning at one of his favorite spots. In a cul-de-sac in an older neighborhood, he had a fine view of the lake.

"I can't get my mind off Zee," he confided to Buffett. "Something bad has happened. I think someone abducted him. I don't want to say that in front of the others. It would be too disheartening. I can see no reason for abducting a homeless person like Zee, other than murder."

Buffett purred as he curled up in Fitz's lap for a nap.

"You'd better not go to sleep before we're through talking. I need your help." Buffett looked up with sleepy green eyes. "That's better. If it were a robbery, why leave all his stuff in the car?"

"Meow."

"You might be right. That gang was after Katía. She and Zee are both Black. What if they are snatching up African Americans? We need to find out if there has been an uptick in kidnapping of African Americans around here. I can't ask the police. They won't cooperate. We'll have to check the newspaper."

"Meow." Buffett stood and rubbed his chin to Fitz's.

"OK. It can wait until after a quick nap." Fitz reclined the back of his seat, put a hat over his eyes, and tried to relax. Buffett kneaded a few biscuits and then was out like a light.

Fitz opened his eyes. It took a moment to orient himself. "I can't believe I actually went to sleep. I thought I was too worried about Zee for that." He let the seat up. "OK, Buffett. Nap time's over."

Buffett stretched and yawned.

"My belly says it's lunch time." He checked his watch. "Right on the button. I say lunch, drive by and check on Zee's car, then hit the library for some research."

Buffett jumped into the back and munched on cat food while Fitz placed an on-line order for a Subway turkey sandwich.

He pulled through the drive-thru, collected his meal, then drove to Walmart. Parking near Zee's car, he unwrapped the sandwich. Buffett sniffed, then gave Fitz a pleading, pitiful look.

"All right." He tore off a piece of the wrapping, pulled out some turkey, and set it on the seat. "Don't make a mess." He rubbed down Buffett's back, then ate his lunch.

A quick check of Zee's car turned up nothing new. Arriving at the library, he scanned the papers for the last week but saw no reports of abductions or murders. Then he started reading on-line articles and lost track of time.

Wow! I've been at this for an hour and a half. I need to check out a book before I go.

He got up and walked the stacks, looking for something that caught his attention. He finally settled on a thriller.

"Sorry I took so long. I got sidetracked," he explained to Buffett, who was awaking from another nap in the sun.

Fitz thumbed through the book. "I hope this is as good as it looks." Setting the book down, he noticed a car passing in front of him.

"Well, look there. An orange Charger. I think we need to find out where they're headed." He hurried out of the parking lot to follow the men who had tried to abduct Katía.

He turned left and followed them till they turned left onto Spring Street. The Charger pulled into a parking space on the left side of the road. Fitz pulled in five spaces down on the right side. The spaces on the one way street were for parallel parking, so he watched out his rearview mirror as the men got out and went into a bar.

"They're starting early, Buffett. I guess they need to get a buzz going for whatever tonight's activities are." *I should let the sheriff's office know where they are. That will be a pleasant call.*

He dialed the sheriff's office, a number he didn't need to look up. "I'm calling in to give the location of suspects wanted in an attempted abduction."

"Could I have your name, please," the lady asked.

It's Geraldine. "This is Joe Fitzgerald, Geraldine. How are you?"

"Is that really you, Fitz? I didn't realize you were still around. What information do you have?"

Fitz explained about the gang members. "The four of them just walked into The Tavern on Spring Street."

"Thanks. I'll forward this to Ron. He might not be happy about the source, though."

"Just tell him to do his job and get someone out here before they leave."

Fitz checked his watch: 4:22pm. "I think we'll stay and keep an eye on them till the police get here," he informed Buffett. He opened the library book and began reading, glancing at the mirror every few seconds.

After three chapters, the light was beginning to fade as the sun slid out of the sky. "I never did like stake out work, Buffett. It's too boring."

By 5:45, it was dark enough that Fitz didn't realize the gang members were leaving the bar till the interior light of their car came on. *I see what Ron thought of my tip.* Bitterness surged in his soul. *I don't think I'll ever be able to forgive them for how they treated me. Apparently, they won't ever forgive me either.*

He let the car pass ahead on the one-way street, then cranked up and followed. The car turned right at the square then right onto Jesse Jewell Parkway. He stayed with them till they pulled off the road near an encampment for homeless folks.

"It looks like they're going to harass some residentially challenged folks, Buffett. Do you think we should put a stop to that?"

"Meow."

Fitz passed the car, turned around down the road a ways, then parked next to a chicken factory. He slid out of the car and donned his Barretta. He could hear the guys tromping through the woods as he approached their car.

He waited by the car till he heard them returning. They were dragging a man along. His hands appeared to be bound behind him. He tried to run once, and one of the guys shoved him to the ground.

Something is wrong. Fitz realized too late that there were only three gang members with the homeless man. *They left one guarding the car.* He heard a twig snap behind him and turned just in time to see a two-by-four swinging toward his head.

Sometime in the night Fitz awoke, shivering in the cold. He touched dried blood on his forehead and remembered the board coming at him. *My car! Buffett!*

Gravity resisted his effort to get off the ground. He finally got to his hands and knees, but when he tried to stand, he fell over. It took two more tries before he was able to stay on his feet. *Man, my head hurts!*

He did a quick inventory of his pockets. *My keys are there, but the gun is gone. What's this?* He pulled a piece of paper out of his coat pocket.

His car was still there, and he was relieved to find Buffett snacking in the back seat. Holding the paper up to the light he read, "Next time you die."

"I'm glad we keep some spares," he said to Buffett as he opened the liftgate and dug down to a lockbox containing three more Berettas and his spare ammunition. "I'm tempted to take out the rat shot."

CHAPTER 13

At 6:45 the next morning. Fitz's phone emitted an unfamiliar sound. *A text?* He was driving toward Laurel Park, having slept in the Walmart parking lot since it was the place closest to where he had been hit in the head.

It was 7:03am when he pulled into the park. Ben was already there. *I was hoping to get the blood cleaned up before he got here.*

He parked and checked the text. "Planning to be there at 7. Ben."

"You're late this morning," Ben chided as Fitz opened his door.

"Yeah. I slept at Walmart last night." He saw shock form in Ben's eyes.

"What happened to your head?"

"I'm pretty sure it was a two-by-four."

"How did you manage to run into a two by four?"

"Actually, it ran into me." He felt the wound again.

"Do you care to explain?" Ben crossed his arms.

"Not really. I need to get cleaned up." It was the pressure to get on with his routine more than wanting to get cleaned up that urged Fitz on.

Fitz winced as he splashed water onto the wound. He winced even more as he tried to rub off the dried blood. *I should have tended to this last night, but it was all I could do to stay conscious long enough to get to Walmart.* He scrubbed some more till the wound became visible.

That probably needs stitches, but a bandage will have to do. He used two band aids to pull the wound together as best he could, having to cut one end of each short to keep them out of his hair. *Maybe that'll hold.*

Exiting the bathroom, he found Ben, Luna, and Katía standing together. They all stared at his forehead.

"What?"

"Are you OK?" Katía asked. "Do you need to see a doctor?"

"It'll heal." He opened the liftgate and carefully stacked his clothes in the dirty clothes spot.

"Who hit you in the head with a two-by-four and why?" Luna asked, hands on her hips.

Fitz saw the determination in her eyes. *They aren't going to stop till I explain.* "Hang on a minute, Buffett."

He closed the liftgate and faced the inquisitors. "I saw the crew that tried to abduct Katía drive by the library, and I followed them. After stopping at a bar, they went to a homeless camp. I watched until they returned. They were dragging someone. I think it was another African American man, but it was dark. The next thing I knew, a two-by-four was crashing into my head. I woke up sometime in the night and slept it off at Walmart."

"You should see a doctor. You might have a concussion," Luna said.

"If I did, they'd just tell me to take it easy, which I plan to do anyway. I'll be fine," Fitz answered.

"Did you report the attack to the police?" Katía asked.

"Oh, please. You know how that would go. I am of the opinion that this Confederate Rising group is behind Zee's disappearance."

"You should at least report that the homeless man was abducted, even if you don't want to report your attack," Ben suggested.

"How am I going to report that? I don't know who the man was. There will be no one else looking for him. They'll just take a report, file it, and be mad that I wasted their time. If these thugs are going to be stopped, I have to do it." Fitz's anger boiled.

"You're wrong, Fitz," Ben said.

"Do you care to explain," Fitz snapped, wondering what Ben meant.

"It's going to take us, not you, to stop these thugs."

"Yeah, we're willing to help. At least, I am. I don't guess I should speak for everyone," Katía added.

"You can count me in. I want Zee back," Luna said.

"So what's next?" Ben asked.

"Next I need to tend to Buffett's water, food, and litter," Fitz replied, feeling the urge to get back to his routine. He opened the liftgate.

"I mean with hunting down this gang." Ben said.

"That's going to be a problem," Fitz answered on his way to fill Buffett's water dish. When he returned with the dish half full of water, he was surprised by the intensity of the faces looking at him. "The problem is that these guys are going to operate at night, so we can't just meet in the mornings and get anywhere."

"I think we all realize that, Fitz," Ben grumped.

"The second problem is that we have no idea where they are going to be. It was just random chance that I spotted them yesterday."

"If we could figure out why they are kidnapping people, we might be able to predict what they're going to do next," Luna suggested.

"I looked them up," Katía added. "Confederate Rising is seeking to create what they call a pure America. They want to bring back the Civil War era idea of colonization and ship anyone who is not White out of the country. They believe that the only way America can be a great nation is if it is a theocracy of White people only."

"So these are supposed to be good Christians who are doing the kidnapping?" Ben asked.

"I guess in their minds they are," Katía answered.

"If we see them again, maybe we should hand them some Bibles," Luna added, drawing a chuckle from Ben and Katía.

Fitz headed to the trash can to dump the litter.

"You don't think they are trying to round up all nonwhite people so they can put them on a boat, do you?" Ben asked.

"That might explain why they were after Katía," Luna noted.

"If that's the case, they would have to be holding them somewhere." Katía observed.

"That's good news," Ben said.

"Why?" Luna asked.

"It means they aren't grabbing them and killing them." The group went quiet. The only sound was Fitz pouring food into Buffett's dish.

"Come on, Buffett. Let's get you suited up. Snickers wants to walk."

With Buffett's harness in place, the group took off down the trail.

"I'll be happy to hold King's leash," Katía offered.

"We need a plan, and we need it quick," Ben said, handing over the leash.

"I wonder if the bar is their regular watering hole," Fitz mused. "Go in, get a little drunk, then go take care of business."

"I bet you're right," Ben said just as Snickers lunged for a squirrel, jerking him forward. "Whoa, girl! You just about pulled my arm out of socket."

"I'll be outside that bar at three-thirty today," Fitz said.

"That's not a good idea," Katía countered. "They'll probably recognize your car."

"That's right. We should take mine," Ben offered.

Fitz pulled a handful of M&Ms out of his pocket and popped a few into his mouth.

"What's wrong, Fitz?" Katía asked.

"Nothing."

"Yes, there is. You always start munching M&Ms when you're stressed."

Fitz grunted. *She's been observing me too closely.*

"Well?" Luna asked.

"Well, what?" Fitz said.

"Are you going to tell us or just clam up?"

I can't tell them the real reason. He came up with a rationalization. "I don't think any of you need to be there. It could be dangerous."

"Obviously. Just look at your head," Ben retorted. "That's exactly why we need to take extra precautions. You and I can go in my car and see what they're up to."

Fitz went silent. The prospect of spending hours in Ben's car was paralyzing. *It makes sense. That's the right move. But can I stand it?*

CHAPTER 14

Fitz pulled into the Publix parking lot to pick up a few items, M&Ms being the most important since he had eaten the rest of his bag that afternoon. He checked the balance in his account and decided he could afford everything on the list.

Working through the aisles, he loaded his reusable shopping bag with a family-size bag of dark chocolate M&Ms, four small cans of chicken, two jars of Alfredo sauce, and four small cans of Buffett's favorite cat food.

He pulled into the new parking deck on Bradford Street at 3:05pm and popped the top on Buffett's canned food.

"That's quite the song you're singing." He put down a dish for the excited cat. "This is because I'm going to be gone for a while. I need you to behave and guard the car, OK?"

Buffett didn't stop eating.

"I'll take that as agreement. This is going to be a rough evening, but I hope we can find Zee." He stroked Buffett's back a few times, the cat's tail rising straight up. Stroking the soft fur was even more calming than the M&Ms. Buffett looked up with approval, then resumed eating.

"What's Katía doing here?" He stopped petting Buffett. He and Ben had agreed to meet at 3:30 to get into position to stake out the bar. "I hadn't planned on her being here. This could be dangerous."

Buffett kept eating. "I see you're not worried." He popped three M&Ms into his mouth.

Katía parked her Prius next to his car. He felt obliged to get out and speak. "What are you doing here?"

"Good afternoon to you, too," she countered.

"I thought it was going to be Ben and me. This might be dangerous."

"That's why I'm here," she said, locking the car from the fob. "I think this calls for all hands on deck. The more people watching, the less chance of being surprised."

"I'd feel more comfortable if I didn't have to worry about you."

Katía put both hands on her hips. "Fitz, we're in this together. We all care about Zee, and this group is too dangerous for you to tackle on your own."

Fitz couldn't think of a response. "I was going to give Ben a gun." He opened the trunk and withdrew one of his spare Berettas.

"Good idea. Let me see that."

Katía checked the safety and popped the clip. Checking the ammo, she slid the clip back in. "It's ready to go."

"I see you know your way around guns."

"Yeah. I grew up in a bad neighborhood. Mom wanted her children to be able to defend themselves, so she taught us how to shoot and fight dirty."

Feeling a bit relieved, Fitz asked, "Do you want a gun, too?"

"No, I'm good." She pulled a Glock G19 part way out of her purse.

Fitz smiled. "A pistol packing pastor. That's not something you see every day." He turned at the sound of a car approaching. It was Ben.

Fitz froze. The time had come. He wasn't happy.

"Whoa, Buffett," Katía said. The cat had hopped into the back of the Highlander, while the liftgate was open. "Maybe you should get things put up before Buffett escapes."

The image of Buffett running away in the parking deck brought Fitz back to action. "Stay put, please." He closed the lock box, returned it to its place, and closed the liftgate as Ben opened his door.

"Hey, Katía. I wasn't expecting you," Ben said.

"I thought the more eyes the better. Besides, I need a little excitement."

Fitz noticed the concern in Ben's eyes. "Don't worry. She knows how to handle herself."

"OK, then. Shall we saddle up and get into position?"

"No Snickers?" Katía asked, looking through the Outback's windows.

"No, I was afraid she might bark."

"Good thinking," Fitz said. "We could take Buffett if you think we need a guard cat on the scene."

Katía laughed. "I don't think Buffett would be much help."

Katía and Ben opened their doors, Katía opting for the back seat. Fitz's feet seemed rooted to the concrete. *This is for Zee. This is for Zee. This is for Zee.* Running that thought over and over freed him to move to get into the car. He took a deep breath and sighed when he closed the door.

"You've got this, Fitz," Katía encouraged.

He popped three more M&Ms into his mouth. "Here, you might need this," he said, offering the gun to Ben.

"What's that for?"

"Your protection. Go around and turn in front of Harrison Tire. Hopefully, we can find a spot just past the bar so they won't see us when they go in."

"You seem confident they'll show up," Ben said.

"If I weren't, I wouldn't be here." *I didn't mean to snap. It just came out that way.*

After an awkward silence, Ben asked, "I wonder why the police haven't caught them yet?"

"Probably because I'm Black and nothing serious happened," Katía replied.

"You don't really think that, do you?" Ben asked.

"I do. The police tend to focus on what's important to them, and a Black woman who didn't get raped or murdered isn't important. Didn't you pick up on the vibes from that deputy? He wasn't interested in my case at all."

"He did seem like a jerk," Ben answered. "I thought it was just because he didn't like Fitz."

"Yeah, that was obvious, too."

"Not all cops are racist, but it does happen to be true of Ron." Fitz pointed up ahead. "That parking place right there."

Ben wiggled the car into the parallel parking place. "Now what?" he asked, cutting the engine.

"You make sure you can see all the way down the street in your rearview mirror, and we wait." Fitz willed his hand to let go of its death grip on the armrest. *I need more M&Ms, but I don't want to look like I'm guzzling them.* He tried to be discreet as he popped the next three into his mouth, but the rattling of the bag sounded loud in the quiet car.

"I guess we might as well chat while we sit here," Katía said. "I know what Fitz did before now. What did you do before you retired, Ben? At least I assume you're retired."

"I was a computer programmer for Feathered Feast, the chicken company."

"So you worked not too far from where I got hit in the head. That homeless camp is on Flat Creek."

"I know where that is, but I usually came and went by Queen City Parkway. I didn't venture over the railroad tracks much."

"Did you like your job?" Katía asked.

"Yeah, for the most part. It could get dull. The best part was when I had new projects to create."

"I have no clue about computer programming. I'm just glad mine works when I turn it on," Katía laughed.

"Lookie there. You were right, Fitz. They just pulled in a few cars behind us," Ben noted.

Katía turned around in her seat.

"Don't turn and gawk, please. They might notice you," Fitz cautioned. Katía turned back around. "It's them, all right."

"Now we wait until they are sufficiently fueled to take on whatever tonight's mission is," Fitz said.

CHAPTER 15

ONE WEEK AGO

Dr. Stanford Cole was seeing his last patient of the day. Betsy Smith's daughter had brought her in for testing because she kept forgetting to take her medicine. The daughter also discovered that Betsy hadn't eaten for several days. That's when she made the appointment.

"Let's give Adlarity a try, Ms. Smith. It's a medicine that helps with memory, and it's a patch so you don't have to remember to take it. You change the patch every seven days. There is a place on the patch to write the date you put the patch on in order to remember when to change it. It might be best if your daughter came over to change the patch. They can be the dickens to get on straight." He gave Betsy his warmest smile.

"Thank you, Doctor, but I don't think I need medicine. I just need to get motivated. My daughter exaggerates, you see."

"The decision is totally up to you, Ms. Smith, but I recommend you at least give it a try. Your test results indicate that you have a need for it. Wearing a patch would be better than ending up in a facility, wouldn't it?" *I hate to play that card, but it usually works.*

He noticed the flash of fear that crossed her face, and his heart sank. *I wish I could tell her this medicine would really prevent that ending.*

Betsy sat stiffly, appearing to mull over his comment. "OK, I'll give it a try. But if it makes me feel bad, I'm taking it off."

"That's a good plan. I'll send the prescription on over to your pharmacy. This says you use Walgreens on Enota. Is that correct?" he asked, scanning her chart on the computer.

"Yes, we do," her daughter said.

Stan returned to his office and crashed into the chair. *There has to be something more effective we can do for these patients. Dementia robs so many people of their lives, of their freedom.*

He sat there stewing in his frustration with the need to get on with his documentation nagging. *I'm tired of waiting to hear back from Herringer.*

He dialed Dr. Herringer's office and explained who he was and the reason for his call to the receptionist. She put him on hold.

When she came back on the line she said, "You're in luck. Dr. Herringer can take your call."

"Hey, Max, this is Stan Cole."

"Good afternoon. It's good to hear from you."

I'm not sure he remembers me. "I'm the neurologist from Gainesville who offered to help with your research."

"I remember who you are, Stan. It's the patients who have dementia, not me. At least not yet," he answered with a chuckle. "What can I do for you?"

"I just had a new dementia patient and am feeling frustrated by not being able to do more to help her. I thought I'd check and see how your research is coming along."

"I'm afraid I've had another setback. The rats just won't cooperate. Trust me, I'll let you know when I'm ready for your assistance." The chuckle had been replaced with icy coldness.

"I'm sorry to hear that."

"Thank you for your interest. Have a good evening." Herringer hung up.

Stan looked at his phone, anger rising at being dismissed so brusquely. He sighed and set into documenting the last visit.

CHAPTER 16

PRESENT DAY

The sun had just set, and the lights bathed the street in an orange glow. The car was starting to get cold after losing the sun's warming rays. Ben stiffened and his hands grasped the wheel. "There they are." He reached to start the car, but Fitz grabbed his wrist.

"Not yet. We don't want to risk drawing their attention. Crank it after they have pulled out of the parking space."

The Charger moved toward the square. Ben pulled out of the parking space to follow.

"Now, don't be in a hurry. Let them stay ahead of us," Fitz coached.

They followed the Charger down Jesse Jewell Parkway. The right turn signal came on.

"Great. They're going to Krystal. Does anyone want a burger?" Fitz said.

"You mean you want me to turn in?" Ben asked.

"Yeah. If they go through the drive-thru, we go through the drive-thru. We'll have to order something."

"I'll take two Krystals, fries, and a Coke," Katía said. She started scrambling in her purse for her wallet.

"Don't you think we'll lose them while we pay?" Ben asked.

"Maybe, but it will look too suspicious if we park and then pull out behind them. I think we have to take the chance," Fitz replied. He noticed his leg had stopped twitching, and he hadn't eaten any M&Ms since they started the chase.

Katía offered her money, but Ben declined. "I've got it. Besides, it will be quicker if we pay with a card." He hit the gas as soon as he got the receipt.

"Perfect. The light's red," Fitz observed. "And they're turning left. I think they're headed back to the homeless camp."

The light turned green before Ben could pull back onto the road. "We're going to lose them," he said.

"Relax. We've got them. Besides, I think I know where they're headed."

The smell of Katía's burger and fries filled the car. "I wish I had ordered some of that," Fitz said.

"I'll share," Katía offered, holding her second burger over the seat.

Fitz hesitated but couldn't resist. "Thanks," he said as he took the burger.

"Don't worry about me. I'm busy driving. I wouldn't be able to eat one of those delicious morsels, anyway," Ben moaned.

"I sure hope you don't starve to death," Katía quipped.

Ben gave a dramatic sigh. "We menial laborers are so overlooked."

"OK, you can have it," Fitz said, setting the burger on the central console.

"Go ahead, Fitz. I was teasing. I'm sure I'll make it."

"I don't want to hear another word," Fitz replied, taking back the burger.

Ben turned left at the light, and they could see the Charger's taillights up ahead.

"I told you we wouldn't lose them," Fitz said.

As the Charger crossed Pearl Nix Parkway, the light turned yellow. "It looks like you're going to have to take back that prediction," Ben said.

"If I'm right, this is perfect. They really won't think we're following them, and we'll find them parked on the side of the road about a quarter of a mile down," Fitz responded. "And if that's the case, I want you to just keep driving like we're not interested at all. We'll make a left turn at Industrial Boulevard and come back and park in the Feathered Feast lot. I assume you're familiar with that spot."

"I know it like the back of my hand," Ben said.

Just as Fitz had predicted, they found the car parked on the side of the road. Three of the men were making their way into the woods.

"Where's the fourth guy?" Katía asked.

"Just keep driving like you're not interested," Fitz coached. "The fourth guy is hiding somewhere to watch the car. That's how I got clobbered."

"I think I see him behind that truck trailer," Katía said.

"Don't slow down," Fitz warned. "We don't want to spook them."

Ben kept driving. As they were turning into the Feathered Feast lot, the far corner of which was diagonally across from where the thugs had headed off into the woods, Fitz instructed Ben to turn off the headlights then pointed to a building up ahead. "Park there and cut the engine. Can you set the cabin lights so they don't come on?"

"I'm sure it can be done, but I have no idea how," Ben answered."

"We don't have time to figure it out. You two stay here, and I'll go see what they're up to." Fitz climbed out of the car to find Ben and Katía standing on the other side. He put his finger to his lips then shut the car door gently, just barely pushing it to. Katía and Ben followed suit.

They crept to the corner of the building and peeked out. Fitz could see the Charger and could just make out two legs under one of the trailers parked just beyond the car. *I should have seen that last time. I'm losing my touch.*

He heard Katía zipping her jacket against the cold. Looking he noticed something black hanging around her neck. "What's that?" he whispered.

"My camera."

"Why?"

"You'll be surprised what this baby can pick up in low light. Don't worry. I turned off all the sensors. It won't give us away."

Since leaving the force seven years ago, Fitz had not really kept up with technology. He had no idea why she would have a camera at night, especially without a flash. *Whatever. I just hope it's quiet.*

They waited in the cold, watching for the men's return. It wasn't long before they heard thrashing in the woods.

"If you want to live, you'd better cooperate," a stern voice ordered. The thrashing continued followed by a clunk. The thrashing stopped, leaving only the sound of footsteps.

"They're carrying someone out," Ben noted.

The one hiding behind the trailer moved to the car and helped drag an unconscious man inside.

Fitz put his finger to his lips. Katía was kneeling on the ground with the camera held in front of her face. Fitz shook his head. He gestured for them to return to the car.

"We have to do something. They're kidnapping that man," Katía whispered as she stood.

Fitz gave her a gentle push toward the car. "We have to be inside before they drive by." Katía resisted. "We'll rescue him at the next stop. We have to find where they're taking these guys. Hopefully, we'll find Zee, too."

Katía relented, and they got into the car, closing the doors just enough to cut the lights.

"Don't put your foot on the brake, and we can't crank it up till they're out of sight," Fitz instructed.

Ben stopped with his foot in midair, habitually going for the brake and ignition. He did as Fitz said, cranking the car once the Charger's lights had disappeared behind him.

Fitz saw the Charger turn left as they pulled onto Dorsey Street. He coached Ben along as they followed about a tenth of a mile behind. The Charger led them into a known gang area a few miles east of Gainesville.

The Charger's left turn signal flashed. "Just keep driving by," Fitz advised. "No, don't slow down!"

It was too late. Ben had not been able to resist slowing down to watch what they were doing and to try to read the number on the mailbox.

"They've made us," Fitz said. "Get out of here!"

"What makes you think they saw us?" Ben asked.

A gunshot answered his question. Ben hit the gas.

CHAPTER 17

Ben turned into the parking lot of a convenience store.

"What are you doing?" Fitz asked.

"I thought I'd stop so we could figure out what to do next."

"I need to report a kidnapping." Fitz turned to see Katía on her phone.

"I've always wondered why we use the word kidnap. It certainly has nothing to do with a child napping," Fitz said.

"The kidnapping was done by the same gang members who tried to abduct me. I can give you the address where they've taken the victim." Katía studied the screen of her camera as she read off the address. "Yes, I'm sure it was an abduction. They knocked the guy unconscious and stuffed him into their car. I hope you will take this seriously and send someone to investigate quickly."

There was a pause as Katía listened. "You should also know they are armed . . . Because they fired at us!"

Katía disconnected the call. "From the way she talked to me, you'd think I was the problem instead of part of the solution."

"Do you mind waiting till the police arrive?" Ben asked. "I'd like to find out if Zee is in that house."

"It looks dilapidated," Katía said, reviewing the footage she had shot.

"You mean you can actually see something on that?" Fitz asked. "I find that hard to believe."

"See for yourself," she said, handing him the camera. "The car lights provided enough illumination. The guys' faces are backlit, so they're not very clear."

"If the deputies bother to come, they will need to see this. What did you get back at the homeless camp?"

Katía took the camera and pulled up the video, stopping it at the point when the guys were stuffing the man into their car. "How's that?"

"Quite incriminating," Fitz answered, handing the camera over to Ben.

"We definitely have to let them see this," Ben agreed. "I hope they find Zee. It's been five days since he disappeared."

It's getting less and less likely we'll find him. Fitz kept that thought to himself. As the wait began to drag on, Fitz's anxiety began to creep back. He dug into his pocket for M&Ms. *I think the worry over Zee is worse than being stuck in this car.* The wait dragged on.

Finally, the flash of blue lights appeared over the hill, followed by sirens blaring. Ben cranked the car.

"We need to give them a minute to get things under control. There might be shooting," Fitz said. He rolled down his window.

After a couple of minutes they heard an authoritative shout, "Hall County Sheriff. Open up." They heard the shout again, followed by silence.

"They must have surrendered," Ben said.

"That's odd. I wouldn't think those guys would go quietly. Let's drive on up," Fitz directed.

Ben parked the car on the side of the road in front of the house. Fitz squinted against the flashing blue lights, shielding his eyes to see what was going on. Deputies were standing around talking. One came hurrying over to the car and knocked on the window.

"I'm sorry, but I have to ask you to leave. This is an active crime scene," He said when Ben rolled down the window.

"We're the ones who reported it," Ben responded.

The officer leaned down and peered into the car. "Fitz. I should have known."

"Ron," Fitz answered. "What did you find in the house? Was Zee there?"

"We found an empty house. If you don't quit wasting our time with these crazy calls, I'm going to arrest you for falsely reporting a crime. Now get out of here." Ron stood and turned.

"I think you need to see the footage my friend shot," Fitz called to Ron's back.

Ron turned around. Fitz could see agitation in his movements. "This had better be worthwhile."

"If you don't find this worthwhile, then you're not much of a law enforcement officer," Katía snarked, rolling down her window. "Press the play button. This is video of the kidnapping we witnessed earlier tonight.

"What does that have to do with this empty house?" Ron said after the video had played.

"Give me the camera and I'll show you." After pulling up the next video, she handed the camera back.

Fitz smiled as exasperation showed on Ron's face. He couldn't resist. "You still think this was a false report?"

"These are the same men who tried to abduct me at the park yesterday. I can't believe you haven't caught them yet."

"They haven't been a high priority," Ron said flatly. "It looks like this was a homeless man they abducted." He handed the camera back to Katía and turned to walk away.

"Don't you want me to send you the videos for evidence?" Katía called.

"If we apprehend them, we'll get in touch. Don't erase them. You people need to leave." Ron walked on back to the other deputies.

"That's one top-notch jerk," Ben said, starting the car.

"It looks like it's going to be up to us to stop this gang," Fitz said.

"Why didn't they catch them?" Katía asked.

"Obviously when they realized we were following them they got spooked and took off. The next question is, 'Did they grab Zee from the house and take him with them?'" Fitz wondered.

"I don't guess there's any way to know," Ben said.

"There might be," Fitz suggested. "How is Snickers's nose?"

"As far as I know, it works just fine."

"Let's bring Snickers and King out tomorrow and see if they seem to recognize a familiar scent."

"Tomorrow's Saturday, so I can come, too," Katía said.

Fitz stuffed three M&Ms into his mouth.

Light had barely begun to emerge over the horizon as Fitz pulled into Laurel Park. He was determined to get there before Ben today. His phone chimed a text alert as he bumped over the speed breaker by the dog park. *Made it.*

It was a full wash day, so he took in the pack of bath wipes and a towel. They were a luxury on which he splurged. *It's so much easier to bathe with these things.* He was packing his dirty clothes into the plastic bag when he heard another car pulling up. It didn't sound like Ben's car.

"It's time to teach this jerk a lesson," Fitz heard through the door. He hurried to get his shoes on. "Let's grab the cat, too."

Leaving his shoes untied, he pulled his gun and cracked the door to peek out. One had a knife about to slash a tire. Another was walking toward the car with a bat.

"I wouldn't advise that," Fitz shouted, stepping out of the bathroom. "And don't even think of reaching for a gun. Down on the ground! All of you!"

The four guys bolted for their car. Fitz almost pulled the trigger. *I can't do it.* He stood frozen, gun aimed at the fleeing car, and watched as the same four guys they had been chasing drove away.

I should have fired. I should have at least shot out a tire. I could have stopped them. Why did I freeze? I'm worthless. He heard tires squeal as they turned out of the park.

CHAPTER 18

Buffett's insistent meow drew Fitz out of his paralysis. He looked to see the cat, paws resting on the door, rubbing his chin on the window, and singing his "I'm hungry" song.

"You're making a fine mess." He eyed the smears on the window then opened the liftgate and began the ritual of feeding Buffett, getting fresh water, and scooping the litter. He was bent over putting the last scoop into the bag when he heard Ben's car pulling in.

He dumped the litter bag into the trash can and exited the bathroom. The lights from Katía's Prius were bouncing over the speed hump. In the east, the sun painted vibrant pink and orange on the canvas of sky.

"Good morning," Ben said as Snickers jumped out of the car and strained on the leash to greet Fitz.

"Mornin'," Fitz replied, leaning down to pet the tail-wagging bundle of energy. "How's your nose today?" he asked the dog. King came over for a pet, too. He seemed sluggish, depressed. "We'll find your buddy soon," Fitz said, stroking the dog's back.

"It was cold last night. Did you do OK?" The wind blew as if emphasizing the point.

"I did run the car a couple of times. Buffett and I are fine."

"I thought you might need a coffee." Ben offered Fitz a warm cup.

"Thanks! That'll hit the spot."

"Hey, guys," Katía chirped, hopping out of her car. "Are we walking or heading straight to the house?"

"I have to walk at least far enough for Snickers to use the bathroom," Ben answered.

Fitz opened the liftgate. "Buffett, do you want to walk?" The cat stayed buried in the sleeping bag on the back seat. "Smart choice." Closing the liftgate, they set off toward the trail. "The goons were already here this morning."

"What happened?" Ben asked.

"I caught them about to slash my tires. They were threatening to snatch Buffett, too."

"I take it you ran them off," Katía observed.

"They don't seem to like the look of my Beretta. I surprised the leader before he had a chance to pull out his gun."

"You didn't report this to the police, I'm guessing," Katía said.

"No." *I didn't want to take the chance of dealing with Ron again.*

Snickers did her business as soon as they got off the concrete. "I think Snickers knows she has work to do," Katía said. Snickers pointed herself toward the car.

"Either that, or she's jealous that Buffett is nice and warm," Fitz added.

"I say we take Snickers's lead and go," Ben suggested. "Come on, King." He gave King's leash a tug so he would follow.

"I think I'll take my car so Buffett can have some heat," Fitz stated.

"Nonsense. Just let Buffett ride with us," Ben said.

Fitz popped three M&Ms into his mouth.

Snickers sat in the back seat like a little lady, watching out the window during the drive. Buffett curled up in Katía's lap and slept. King sat in the back of the car, whining.

"Traitor," Fitz scolded. Buffett ignored him and purred contentedly.

As Ben pulled into the driveway, Fitz slipped out his gun. "Let's sit and wait a minute to see if they're here. They'll probably come out after us if they are."

Snickers whined at the window, then hopped into the front, crowding Fitz while Ben attached her leash. Buffett turned and resettled in Katía's lap.

"I don't think anyone's here," Katía said.

The urge to get out of the car won, and Fitz opened the door. "Let's go."

Snickers bounded out of the car and sniffed around while Ben leashed up King. The small white house had a concrete stoop accessed by three steps. Snickers kept sniffing as Ben led her to the front door. King perked up, sniffing the stoop with zeal.

"Do you think they're smelling Zee's footprints?" Fitz asked.

"It's hard to tell. She always does this in a new place," Ben answered.

Snickers hopped off the stoop and stood alert, giving one bark. "What have you found?" Ben asked, going to join her. "Good dog!" he said, showering her with pets. "Hey guys! Look what Snickers found."

Fitz and Katía joined them, looking down to see a treat like Zee always kept in his pocket. King remained on the stoop, sniffing and whining.

"Way to go, Snickers!" Katía said, administering her own pets. She whipped out her camera and snapped a few photos.

"I think we can say Zee was here," Ben said.

"Or the former residents had a dog and dropped one there," Fitz pointed out.

"This is way too fresh to have been dropped by former residents," Katía noted.

Snickers whined, eyes locked on the treat. "Go ahead. You can have the treat, Snickers," Fitz said.

"Wait! That's evidence. Shouldn't we call the police?" Katía asked.

"Like that will do any good," Fitz retorted. "They don't care about this case, especially Ron. If they did, our little gang wouldn't still be running around grabbing folks."

"You do have a point," Ben said. "If we could find them, then why couldn't they?"

"So… you don't think they are even trying to find Zee?" Katía asked.

"I really don't," Fitz answered. "He's homeless for one and African American for a second. That equates to Ron's not being willing to lift a finger."

"That's just sick. What about the rest of the sheriff's department?" Katía asked.

"I wouldn't be surprised if Ron never put the word out that Zee was missing. He might not even have filed the reports of our calls, but that would be a brazen breaking of the law."

Katía's hands went to her hips, and her posture stiffened. "I'm going straight to the sheriff, then. This kind of apathy and discrimination is not going to happen in my county. Let's go so I can give Sheriff Tucker a piece of my mind!"

"I can think of at least one problem with that," Fitz said.

"What?" Katía snapped, turning after already starting toward the car.

"It's Saturday."

Snickers looked from Katía to Ben to the dog biscuit and whined. "What is it, girl?" Ben stooped to look at the treat. "So it's OK to give it to her?"

"She found it. I think she deserves a reward," Fitz answered.

Ben picked up the biscuit and turned it over. "I think this will quell any doubts." He held it up, revealing a Z scratched into the underside.

CHAPTER 19

Why can't I make them understand me? I'm speaking as plain as day. He sat on the side of the bed in the small room that had become his prison. There was no window and no clock. He had no idea what time of day it was.

They won't even let me walk around. The men bring me food three times a day. I ask them what's going on and when I can leave. They just laugh. One has taken to asking me questions. Maybe he just wants to hear me talk. I don't think I have a funny accent or anything.

"Hey! I want to get out of here! When can I leave?" he yelled.

"Shut up!" one of the workers responded, walking on by.

What am I going to do? I have to get out of here. If I could find a phone, I'd call the police. Maybe I can sneak out tonight.

Since they weren't watching him, he rubbed the sore spot on his head. *Why is my head shaved? It itches. Are those stitches?*

"Boss, we found another one who seems to have dementia," he heard coming from the hallway.

"How can you tell with a rat like that?" was followed with a chuckle. "Let's save it for later. Show me the one you say doesn't make sense when he talks."

The usual worker and a well-dressed man stepped through the door. The well-dressed one pulled the chair over next to him and sat down.

"Good morning. Sorry to bother you this early in the day, but I wanted to see how you are feeling," the well-dressed one said.

"My head hurts, and I want to get out of here. You can't hold me against my will. That's illegal."

The man's forehead scrunched up as he looked to the worker. "Let's try something simple. Tell me your name, just your first name."

"Josiah."

He looked to the worker again. "Can you say the letter A?"

"A. Now let me leave."

The man pulled out an electronic gadget and pressed it to Josiah's chest. "Hmmm," he said, studying the gadget. "I'm going to turn it off. Let me know how he is tomorrow."

He fidgeted with a couple of buttons then held the thing back to Josiah's chest.

"Have a good day." He stood and slid the chair back against the wall.

"Please let me leave. I'm tired of being here."

The two walked out of the room, and as they walked down the hall, Josiah heard, "If this doesn't work, we might have to terminate his trial."

CHAPTER 20

Fitz looked over the biscuit carefully. "That was no accident. At least we can be sure Zee was here. We're on the right trail, and I hope he's still alive." Fitz sensed faint rush of hope stir in the group.

"I think we need to keep this for evidence," Katía said, holding out her hand.

"Sorry Snickers," Fitz said, depositing the biscuit into Katía's hand.

"Now what?" Ben asked.

"That's a good question," Fitz replied, stroking his long beard. "I wonder…" He walked up to the door and turned the knob. "Unlocked. Let's check it out." He pulled out his Barretta as he opened the door.

"Katía pulled out her Glock and followed.

"What is this? Should I get the gun you loaned me out of the car?"

"Come on," Katía whispered. Ben, Snickers, and King followed.

Walking into the dark house, Fitz paused to let his eyes adjust, listening on high alert. He held his hand back, signaling the others to wait. Hearing no sound, he proceeded on.

The living room was empty except for a few granola bar wrappers littering the floor. Fitz moved on to a bedroom. He pointed to a chain with a shackle that was attached to the dumpy twin bed.

Snickers and King strained on their leashes, whining and pulling toward the other bedroom.

"What is it, girl?" Ben asked. They followed the dogs.

King sniffed around the bed and barked. "I think this is where they held Zee," Ben said. There was another chain attached to the bed.

"I'm calling the police," Katía said. "They have to know about this." She pulled out her phone and dialed 911.

Fitz popped M&Ms into his mouth. "I hope Ron's not pulling a double shift. They should have seen this last night."

"I want to make sure," she replied.

After the call, she aimed her camera and began taking shots of the chain, bed, bedside table, and discarded granola bar wrappers. There was a mug on the bedside table. She moved to the next bedroom and continued photographing.

Fitz checked the fridge. "This is empty. It looks like their chains were long enough to get to the bathroom. I'm guessing all they had was granola bars and water."

Opening another door, Fitz found the same setup in a third bedroom. "This one doesn't appear to have been used, unless the goons did a cleanup job."

Katía photographed that room, too.

"You should have been a crime photographer," Ben suggested.

"Nah. I don't think that was my calling." She checked her watch.

"Do you have somewhere to be?" Ben asked.

"I have a couple more hours. Some folks from our church are taking food to the homeless camp at eleven."

"Are you nuts? You've seen what's happening there," Ben said.

"The good news is that the CR men are probably holed up somewhere sound asleep this time of day," Fitz stated.

"Don't they have to work?" Ben asked.

"They probably work by stealing and selling drugs. Judging from this set up, they're probably getting paid for their abductions."

"What could they be doing with these men?" Katía asked.

"I have no idea unless it's a human trafficking scheme. It seems to be African American men they are after," Fitz replied.

"Except they also tried to capture me," Katía reminded him.

Fitz heard gravel crunching and looked out to see an SUV from the sheriff's office pulling in. He popped three more M&Ms into his mouth.

A young officer whom Fitz didn't know got out. He breathed a sigh of relief.

"Hi, I'm Jeremy Stancil. I got a call about suspicious activity here."

Katía stepped up. "I'm Katía Bancroft. I placed the call. I wanted to make sure your office had a record of the chains that were holding people prisoner here."

"That sounds bad. Let's take a look. And you're?" Jeremy asked, holding his hand out toward Ben.

"Ben Blessing. It's nice to meet you."

"Next," Jeremy said with a smile.

"Fitz Fitzgerald. Thanks for coming."

"Oh. The Fitz? I've heard a lot about you. Let's see what you've found."

More M&Ms.

Katía hurried to the front door.

"Wait, is this your house?" the deputy asked.

"No. It's a place where a friend of ours was being held prisoner," she answered.

Her words drew a disapproving look from the deputy. "What, might I ask, were you doing in a house that doesn't belong to you?"

"We are trying to find our friend who we believe has been kidnapped by the Confederate Rising gang," Katía fumed.

"You should have called us before you went in," Jeremy scolded.

"Just go and look," Fitz said from behind. "This should have been in the report, but we wanted to make sure it wasn't missed."

"What report?" Jeremy asked.

"Weren't you briefed about the call to this house last night?" Fitz asked.

"Nope.

"What? No report?"

Jeremy scowled at Fitz. "If I had been briefed, would I have said I hadn't?"

"Interesting," Fitz said, stroking his beard.

"What's interesting?"

"We placed a call last night regarding the abduction of a homeless person. The gang members brought him here. Apparently they realized we had followed them and took off before the deputies got here. I would think that would be significant enough to be brought up at report."

"Ron would have told me had that happened."

"It happened. All three of us were here. I even showed him videos of the abduction," Katía chimed in.

"All I can say is this is the first I've heard of it."

"Interesting," Fitz said again.

"This is probably illegal since I don't have a search warrant, but let's see what you've found."

Katía led the way into the house and pointed out the chains and shackles attached to the beds.

"This definitely looks like a human trafficking set up," Jeremy mumbled. "Please tell me you haven't touched anything."

"Just our shoes on the floor," Fitz answered.

"Hold on a minute. I need to look up some things on my computer. And I'll need you to wait outside."

Following Jeremey outside, Katía said, "There's more. We found a dog treat like the ones our friend always carries. It has his initial scratched onto it." She held out the biscuit.

Jeremy grunted and walked to his vehicle.

"Do you think he believes us?" Katía asked.

"I do. It seems he's not happy that Ron didn't brief him on the situation. That sounds like Ron, though."

Katía checked her watch. "I'm still good."

"What's our next move?" Ben asked.

"We need to find where they took them, obviously. But how?" Katía answered.

CHAPTER 21

Katía was two minutes late, arriving at 11:02am. Shirley, Adrienne and Hope were waiting outside.

"Hey! Sorry I'm late," Katía said, hurrying out of her car. "Have y'all been waiting long?"

"Just long enough to talk about you," Adrienne quipped, offering a mischievous grin.

Katía laughed. "I trust it was good."

"We'll never tell," Shirley chided.

"I'll be happy to drive," Katía offered.

"Where would we put the food? Your car is so little," Hope, the owner of the Yukon parked next to Katía's Prius, said.

"I have a trunk… or whatever you call the back of a hatchback. It'll work."

"OK, honey, but you might have to pry me out of it," Hope laughed. The large SUV suited Hope's size better. They loaded their collection of sandwiches, canned food, homemade brownies, and can openers into the back of Katía's car.

"Let's have a prayer before we take off," Katía said. "Dear Lord, we are grateful for every opportunity you give us to serve you and our fellow human beings. Please bless these gifts and use them to enrich the lives of the people who eat them. Amen."

Hearty Amens echoed through the group, then they got into the car.

"How ever did you find a homeless camp?" Adrienne asked.

Katía paused, trying to frame her answer. "I learned about it from an unhoused person I met at the park." *That was both not a lie and true. Nailed it!*

"I think it's a great idea. Maybe we could do this on a regular basis," Hope said.

"We definitely should," Shirley agreed.

"Sounds good to me, as long as we're out of there before it gets dark," Adrienne added.

A nervous chill ran down Katía's back as she pulled in and parked in the same place the gang members had.

"Where's the camp?" Adrienne asked.

"I'm not sure. It's down in the woods that way, somewhere," Katía answered.

"In the woods?" Shirley gasped.

"Yeah, but I'm sure it's not far. Just think of it as a nice hike."

A well-worn path led away from the road, so Katía followed it as it meandered along a creek. It wasn't long till she saw tents up ahead.

"Hello," she called, nerves tightening as they approached. "Hello. We have food to share."

A woman's wary face poked out of a tent. With leathery skin and greying brown hair, the woman appeared on high alert. "What do you want?" she growled and gradually pushed a baseball bat through the tent door.

The four women stopped. Hope stepped around into the front. "Don't be threatening me with a bat. I'll snap you and the bat in two so fast you won't know what hit you. We're bringing food if you care for any. We've got homemade brownies."

"Hope!" Katía scolded, then watched as the woman's posture relaxed.

"Pardon the bat. We got to be careful 'round here." She stepped out of her tent and yawned. "Sorry. You woke me up. You mentioned food?"

The four women approached, shopping bags in hand. "We have sandwiches, canned goods, and brownies, as Hope mentioned," Katía explained. "We were hoping y'all could use some."

"Is anyone else around?" Adrienne asked.

"I think everybody's at Good News at Noon for lunch."

A sudden snore sounded from one of the tents. "Except Charlie. It sounds like he's still sleeping off last night's activity."

"How many people live here?" Shirley asked.

"Don't know. Never counted."

Shirley counted the tents. "There are a dozen tents. I'm assuming one person per tent?"

"That sounds right. Ain't nobody shacking up here."

"I guess we could divvy up the food and leave it in the tents. We only brought 6 can openers, though," Adrienne suggested.

"Most of us have can openers. I can hold them and give them out to anyone who doesn't," the woman said.

While Hope, Adrienne, and Shirley started dividing up the food, Katía talked to the woman. "My name's Katía. What's yours?"

"They call me Sarge."

"Sarge, huh?" Katía raised an eyebrow.

"It's because I don't take no crap around here."

"Do you have any trouble in the camp?"

"Sometimes the guys will get high and get to fightin'. That's when I get out Betsy," she said, patting the bat.

"Any trouble the last few days?" Katía asked, hoping to hear about the kidnapping.

"Yeah. Twice, some goons came through the camp shining flashlights in our eyes. They dragged off one guy each time. Both Black guys."

"They didn't hurt anyone else?"

"Nah. If we wasn't Black, they moved on."

Why didn't you go to Good News at Noon for lunch?"

"I sleep during the day so guys can't surprise me at night when they're feeling amorous."

"It sounds like a hard life," Katía replied, the weight of Sarge's situation pressing on her heart. "Isn't there a shelter or something you could get into where you'd be safer?"

"Maybe. But I likes me a bit of weed here and there," Sarge whispered.

"How can you afford to buy marijuana?" Katía asked.

"Now that would be a trade secret, wouldn't it? Thanks for the food. It's not often we get good folks comin' through."

Food distributed, the women folded their bags. "Charlie never even stirred," Shirley said.

They waved good-bye to Sarge and headed back toward the road. After a few steps, they heard, "You'd better be careful. Your type is who those goons are after."

Sarge's comment sent a chill down Katía's spine. *You don't know how right you are.* "Are there any more Black people in the camp now?" she called back.

"Nah. Those creeps cleared 'em out."

"You be careful and take care of yourself," Katía said as they resumed their trek toward the car.

"I bet she's going to sell those can openers," Hope griped.

"More power to her," Adrienne replied.

When the road came into sight, Katía stopped. A Charger passed by, but it wasn't a low-rider. *I'm getting jumpy.*

"What is it?" Shirley asked.

"Nothing. I was just looking around. I guess there are worse places to live." She took off in a hurry.

CHAPTER 22

Fitz decided he would sleep at Walmart that night to keep an eye on things just in case. Leaving the library, where he had been reading, he fancied a hot meal. *A burger and fries sure would hit the spot. It's a shame Collegiate is already closed. I guess I'll hit Wendy's.*

Going through the drive-thru, he ordered a double burger with ketchup, mustard, pickles, lettuce, and tomato, and fries and a medium Coke. He paid, collected his food, and scanned the section of the Walmart parking lot where homeless folks usually parked.

"Buffett, where would be the best place to park to keep an eye on my residentially challenged compadres?"

Buffett meowed and rubbed Fitz's chin. "I should have known you wouldn't be able to make a decision with the aroma of hamburger in the air. It's always belly first with you. OK, let's eat before it gets cold."

Buffett seemed to understand and sat politely in the passenger seat while Fitz dismantled the hamburger and tore up one of the patties. "There you go. Bon appétit!"

The two happily munched on their food as the sun began setting. "I'm smarter than I thought I was. We have a front row seat for the sunset."

With supper consumed, Fitz drove to the closest parking place he could find near Walmart. "I'll be back in a bit, buddy. I'm going to take advantage of their warm facilities."

After using the restroom, he lingered by the counters near the registers. *I shouldn't. But I want to. Heck, you only live once.* He gave in to the temptation and purchased a Midnight Milky Way bar.

Back at the car, he opened the door. "Wow, Buffett! I wish you had waited till I had eaten my candy bar before you did that." He checked the litter box to make sure Buffett's deposit was fully covered. "You did a good job. I guess we just wait a bit. What am I thinking? They have trash cans here."

After scooping the litter, he selected a parking spot that afforded him a view of the several cars he knew belonged to the residentially challenged. "This ought to work."

He worked his way into the sleeping bag. "I think I'll read a bit. What do you want to do?"

Buffett crawled into his lap and curled up while Fitz leaned over and pulled a headlamp out of the glove box. "I wonder if you get bored being stuck in this car."

Buffett purred. "OK. I guess you're satisfied." He opened "Dark Wings Rising," the book he'd checked out, and read till he became sleepy.

It was just a quick yelp, but it was enough to disturb his sleep. It took a minute for Fitz to awaken enough to realize what he'd heard. Opening his eyes, he saw the orange Charger driving away.

"Buffett, we have to go!" Not having time to get out of the sleeping bag, he unzipped the bottom to let his feet out and cranked the car. "This'll have to do." Without turning on the headlights, he followed.

The Charger turned left out of Walmart. Fitz stayed back, turning on his headlights just before making the left out of the parking lot. It was the middle of the night, and very few cars were out.

The Charger surged forward and tires squealed as it ran the red light and turned left onto Dawsonville Highway. *If I run the light, they'll know I'm following them. I have to take my chances and stop. They might already know, which would explain why they took off.* He watched the Charger as it kept going straight and out of sight.

He pounded his hands on the steering wheel, and Buffett jumped. "Sorry."

It seemed the light would never turn. Fitz was tempted to run it. Just as he was about to go, the yellow light came on for the other direction. When he saw green, he accelerated, going under the next light just as yellow turned to red. *They're going to keep changing.* He kept pressing the accelerator a little harder.

He was going sixty-six miles per hour when he passed under the light at McEver Road. *Maybe I can catch them.* His burst of optimism was squashed by blue lights coming behind him. *Great! Just what I need. No good deed goes unpunished.*

He slowed down and pulled over, trying to get control of his emotions so his tongue wouldn't get him into even worse trouble. *What a pleasant surprise.* The patrol car passed him and kept going down the road.

"Now what, Buffett? Is there any point in going on?"

"Meow."

"You're right. They might be after the guys in the Charger." Fitz pulled out and kept going, keeping an eye on his speedometer.

He continued on, crossing the bridge over Lake Lanier. There was still no sign of the Charger when he reached Sardis Road.

"Well, buddy, I think we might as well give up the chase." He made a U turn and drove back to Walmart.

"It's right toasty in this sleeping bag after running the heat that long," he explained to Buffett.

"Meow."

"I know. You like it toasty. Crawl on back in." Buffett nestled down into the sleeping bag to finish out the night.

The light touch of a cat paw awakened Fitz. He checked his watch. "Six o'clock sharp. How do you do that?" Buffett had been waking up Fitz at six for a long time. He was as reliable as an alarm clock.

He pulled out the treat bag and delivered six treats to the passenger seat. While Buffett gobbled those down, Fitz stretched back till he located his bag of Cliff Bars. After selecting a chocolate chip one, he returned the bag to its place.

"I sure would like a hot cup of coffee. Do you think I could get away with it here?" he asked Buffett. No response as Buffett continued eating. "Well I'm going to try anyway."

He set up the PocketRocket stove on the asphalt next to the car. He hopped back in to stay warm while the water boiled, keeping an eye out for police as he scooped instant coffee into his cup.

Cutting off the stove, he poured the hot water into his cup, dumped the excess, and set the pot back on the stove to cool. "Mission accomplished without getting caught," he told Buffett. Buffett stretched and hopped into the passenger seat, sniffing to see if he might like some of what was in the cup. "Nope. You wouldn't like this."

At precisely 6:30, Fitz cranked the car and headed to the park. "Right on schedule." On the way his phone signaled a text message. *I guess I'd better get used to that.*

Ben and Luna pulled in right behind each other, parking a couple of spaces from Fitz. They exchanged greetings.

"It was another cold one last night. Did you do OK?" Ben asked.

"You can stop worrying about us. We handle the cold just fine."

"You did run the car to warm it up, didn't you?" Luna pressed.

"Not by choice."

"What do you mean?" Ben asked.

"The gang hit the Walmart lot again. I woke up and tried to follow them, but they got away."

"This is ridiculous!" Luna said, anger flaring. "We have to do something to stop them. We have to find Zee." Her hands went to her hips. "I don't guess there's any point in asking if you reported this to the police."

"You're right. I didn't. They're obviously not interested in what's happening to homeless Black folks."

"They weren't interested in what happened to Katía, either," she fumed.

"We need to spread the word about what's going on to everywhere there are homeless folks," Ben said.

"We really need to let every African American in town know, but I don't know how we could do that," Luna added.

"I know how we could reach a few of them," Ben said. "I'll text Katía and ask her to announce what is going on to her church this morning." He pulled out his phone and started texting. "Why don't we meet at my house after church for grilled cheese sandwiches? I'll print up some fliers and we can deliver them. Say twelve-thirty-ish?"

"That works for me. My husband can manage on his own today," Luna answered.

Fitz didn't respond.

"How about you, Fitz? Are you coming?"

"You don't want me in your house."

"Nonsense. I would love for you to be there. I'll text everyone the address."

CHAPTER 23

Max Herringer's secretary patched a call through. "Hello, this is Doctor Herringer," he answered.

"Hey, Doc. The last one's awake and acting normal."

"You're talking about subject A7? What's it doing?"

"Walking around. Eating. Seems to be the same as before the procedure."

"That's good news," the flatness of his tone belying his growing excitement. "Maybe the change in positioning was the trick… You did turn on the device at the right time, correct?"

Max frowned at the expletives hitting his ears. "I'll take that as a no," he said. "Correct your mistake and turn it on now, then give me a report after lunch."

"Yes, sir. Sorry."

"Never mind about the report. I'm coming out there this afternoon." He hung up the phone gently, trying to squelch the rage he was feeling. *This has to work. Max Herringer doesn't fail.*

That last thought was true. A childhood prodigy, he had failed at nothing he attempted. Graduating first in his class from high school, college, and medical school, he had always excelled. He had never set his hand to a research project that didn't succeed. He had not become a world-famous neuroscientist by giving up on a project, and he wouldn't this time. *I will find a way to make this work.*

Eating lunch at his desk, he pored over strategy options for the procedure he was trying to develop. He went over and over the MRIs of the electrode placements. *I think the initial ones failed because they were too close to Wernicke's area. Surely I didn't hit it.* He studied the images more closely.

No, but it is close. He pulled up A7's MRI. *This one is definitely more centrally positioned. I shall cross my fingers and hope for satisfactory results.* He shut down his laptop, put it into its case, and headed for the lab.

Punching in the code, he opened the lab door. "How's A7 doing?"

"He can't stop puking. It's disgusting. Puked all over the place."

"Get it cleaned up. Let's give Phenergan and see what happens. It could be the anesthesia." Max was not a fan of barf. It turned his stomach in a hurry. He elected not to examine at this time. *At least they're expendable.* "How about A6? Any improvement?"

"Nah. Still bat crazy."

"I see. We'll give it a couple more days before we terminate."

"We're going to need that space for new ones soon."

"I said give it a couple more days. I want to see what happens," Max snapped.

CHAPTER 24

Fitz parked on the street in front of Ben's house and ate five M&Ms. The house was a brick two-story home, nice but not extravagant. He reached for the Highlander's door handle, but his hand stopped like an invisible wall was blocking it. *I don't think I can do this.*

It had been a long time since he had been inside a house. He had grown comfortable with interacting casually with people at the park, but this was getting too close. He tried to remember the last time he was at a house.

It was Steve's house. I went to see him right before he died of cancer. That was three days after I became residentially challenged. Bad associations with houses.

Buffett meowed and hopped into the back. "So you say it's lunch time. Do you think I should go in?"

"Meow."

"OK." He chewed three more M&Ms and headed for the door. Ben opened it before he got there, cutting off any chance of changing his mind.

"Hey, Fitz! Come on in!"

He said it like this was a normal thing. I guess for most people it is. He walked in, slipping three more M&Ms into his mouth while Ben closed the door.

"Hey, Fitz," Luna called from the kitchen counter where she sat on a bar stool. "I've found one other homeless camp and five shelters we need to visit. I didn't tell my husband I would be running around with two other men this afternoon," she laughed.

"Hey," Fitz replied, not knowing what else to say about her comment.

"Make yourself at home, Fitz. I'm going to start the grilled cheese sandwiches," Ben said.

Ben was a widower, having lost his wife to cancer four years ago. His only child lived three hours away. *Having people over is probably important to him.* Fitz tried to wrangle his discomfort into something positive.

"If you keep eating M&Ms, you won't be hungry for lunch," Luna noticed.

"Yes, ma'am," Fitz said, cheeks turning red.

"I think we should hit the shelters first and then try to find this other camp. I assume the one Katía went to is already aware. I haven't figured out how to get to the other camp, though," she said.

"I know where it is," Fitz offered. "I guess Katía is busy today." He found himself worrying about her, which was a new thing for him. A knock at the door startled him.

"Would somebody answer that? It's time to flip the sandwiches."

Luna didn't budge from her phone, so Fitz headed to the door.

"Hey! Am I too late?" Katía bubbled.

"We thought you'd be too busy today."

"I'm never too busy to help folks in trouble." She patted Fitz on the shoulder and popped on in. "I'm still wound up from preaching."

Fitz followed her into the kitchen. "There might not be any administrative types at the shelters. I guess we could tape something onto the door."

"The fliers I made are on the table. Show them, Luna," Ben said from the stove.

She passed out the fliers. Fitz scanned the paper, seeing two pictures of the Charger, one showing the license plate. It read, "BEWARE! The men driving this vehicle are abducting African Americans. They are particularly targeting homeless people but have shown they will go after anyone in an isolated setting. PLEASE BE CAREFUL!"

"That's perfect! I announced it at church this morning and told everyone to pass the word." Katía said.

Ben set a plate of sandwiches on the table. Chips and pickles were already there. "We have water, tea, and sodas to drink. Take your pick."

With lunch consumed, including Luna's homemade cookies, they headed to Ben's car. "You have to stay home," Ben instructed Snickers. She and King sat, looking forlorn.

"Maybe I should just follow you," Fitz said.

"Nonsense. That would be a waste of gas," Katía scolded. As they pulled out, Fitz noticed Buffett asleep on the dash in the sunshine.

They taped fliers onto the doors of My Sister's Place, Gainesville Baptist Mission, Salvation Army, Good News at

Noon, and Family Promise. Then Fitz directed them to the camp.

"Take this first entrance into the shopping center. We're going to park behind the stores."

When Ben parked, Fitz jumped out of the car, relieved to be free of the confining space.

"Which way do we go?" Luna asked.

"I haven't ever been here. Look for a path." Fitz answered.

They spread out and started searching.

"Hey, guys. I think I found it." They followed Ben's eyes to see a skinny White man walking into the woods. The man noticed them and quickened his steps.

"Do you have your gun, Katía?" Fitz asked.

"Of course. I've had it with me ever since they tried to snatch me."

"Gun?" Luna asked. "I wasn't expecting danger. I thought we were just handing out fliers."

"It'll be fine. I just want to be prepared," Fitz said to comfort her.

"Interesting. A preacher who carries a gun," Luna mused.

"I don't plan on killing anyone. It's mostly a deterrent. In fact, I have snake shot in the first chamber."

Fitz burst out laughing. "You've got to be kidding. I do, too."

"I knew we were kindred spirits," Katía laughed.

They made their way down the path till they saw tents up ahead.

"Hello!" Katía called. "We've come to bring news..."

The bean pole of a man they had seen earlier stepped into the path, blocking their way. He crossed his arms and glared. "You folks don't belong here."

"We didn't come to stay," Luna said. "We just want to warn you about some dangerous people. What's your name?"

"They call me Captain. We don't take kindly to strangers."

"If you'll move and let us distribute some fliers, we'll be on our way," Fitz said.

Captain tilted his head. "Fitz? Is that you?"

"Yeah. It's me."

"It's Roy. Roy Rollins."

"Great goat guts! I never would have recognized you. You've lost so much weight."

"Shut up. Not a lot to eat lately. At least my beard isn't as scraggly as yours. How long has it been?"

"I haven't seen you since I was discharged," Fitz said, stepping forward to shake his hand. "This is Roy. He and I were in the army together. He earned his title of Captain."

"From what I heard, you did, too. I guess we'll let you guys come visit." He ushered them into the camp like he was welcoming them to church, introducing the three men who poked their heads out of their tents. "Now, what brings folks like you to our humble abode? These three clearly don't belong on the streets, Fitz. You could pass, though," he laughed.

"There are four men who are going around abducting people. They seem to be targeting Black folks," Katía explained. "They drive this car." She gestured to Ben who handed over one of the fliers."

"Yeah, I've heard about these jerks."

"You have?" Luna asked, surprise in her eyes.

"Yeah. Word gets around. We talk, you know." He studied the picture. "I saw that car today in the parking lot while I was working it. They were filling a cooler with beer. Low-rider, right?"

"Yeah," Ben answered. "What do you mean, you were working the parking lot?"

"You need to get out more. I was seeking donations, man. On Sundays people are usually in a generous mood, especially the church folks. You can see their guilt complex kick in when they're trying to decide whether to donate to the cause." He pulled a sandwich from his pocket. "I got enough for this today. I'll have the other half tomorrow. Eatin' good in the hood, baby!"

"Captain, would you mind if we leave these fliers for folks?" Fitz asked.

"People don't take kindly to their homes being invaded. I can hand them out."

Ben was already handing them out to the three onlookers.

"Are there any Black folks here?" Katía asked.

"We got one guy."

"He'll be the one they're after." Katía said. "Which one is his tent?"

Captain jutted his chin toward a camouflage tent set off a ways.

"Don't watch. I'm going to slip this inside," she said.

"So you think this is a serious threat?" Captain asked, eyes on Fitz.

"They already got three people that we know of. One was a friend. They tried to abduct her at the park early one morning." Fitz gestured toward Katía.

"How did she get away?"

"My Beretta convinced them to back down. Are you armed?"

"No. Had to pawn my gun a long time ago."

Fitz opened his mouth but stopped. *If I give him a gun, he'll just sell it.* "I'd advise finding a big stick, then."

CHAPTER 25

A plan formed in Fitz's mind as he drove away from Ben's house. "Buffett, we're going to do another stakeout tonight. It'll be risky, but I know just the place to park. First there's the matter of supper. Ben served us grilled cheese for lunch. Maybe I'll just do beans and rice for supper."

He headed to Sardis Creek Park, which was on the way from Ben's house to the shopping center they had visited earlier. He set up his PocketRocket stove on the picnic table, added black beans, rice, and water to the pot, then ignited the stove. Buffett sniffed around, his leash looped around the seat.

"Except for the breeze, it would be nice out today." Buffett didn't respond. "I know. It doesn't bother you with your fur coat."

The sun was sitting low in the sky, threatening to withdraw its warmth. The air carried the smell of the lake. Fitz pulled her picture up on his phone. Looking into her lovely eyes, he said, "I wish I had been with you that day. We could have died together. Then I wouldn't have been stuck alone like this."

He stared at all he had left of the love of his life. Sharon had been career army, too. They had met in a bar when stationed at the same location for a few days. She had been the one with the pick-up line, and Fitz fell hard for her.

They continued to rendezvous on leaves and when their paths crossed. Their army careers made marriage too difficult a proposition, so they agreed to be lovers and be married in spirit if not in truth. She was killed by a roadside bomb in Iraq.

A good therapist would probably tell me I need to move on and quit looking back. I'm just not ready to let go.

The timer he had set for his meal went off. "Have I been looking at you that long? I have to go now. Bye."

He wiped a tear from his cheek and turned off the stove. "Come on, Buffett. I'm getting back into the car."

Buffett sniffed Fitz's pot of beans and rice. "You wouldn't like it even if I gave you some so give up the idea. You need to help me get my mind off Sharon."

Buffett nuzzled his chin. "Thanks."

Fitz pulled into the shopping center parking lot at 6:42pm. It was dark and empty except for a few employee cars. Things closed up early on Sundays. He made his way around behind the shopping center and backed in next to a dumpster he had noticed earlier.

He located his headlamp and book. "Let me know if you see any headlights coming," he instructed Buffett.

"Meow." Buffett curled up in his lap and purred.

"I don't think you're going to be much help." Trying to banish Sharon's ghost, he turned to the book.

A couple of hours later, the sensation of light awoke him. He didn't remember falling asleep. A surge of panic hit, and he reached for the headlamp. *I don't remember turning you off, either.* Confused, he looked out the window. Lights were bobbing up and down along the line of trees at the edge of the asphalt. He ducked down as best he could when one came in his direction.

"Ain't nothin' this way," a voice called.

"What makes you think there's a camp here?" another voice said.

"Research, you idiot. Keep looking. There's bound to be a path somewhere."

My hunch was right. Do I let them find the camp? They might hurt Roy. If I don't let them keep going, I might not ever find Zee. The conflict sparked anger. The more he thought about the situation, the madder he got. Then a solution struck. *This is probably a bad idea.*

As he reached for the door handle, a light appeared to his right. He paused and watched as a vehicle approached. *The police.* Looking to his left, he could see the flashlights moving quickly toward a car. It was the Charger. Blue flashing lights strobed the scene. *They're going to run.*

Sure enough, the Charger came to life and sped around the corner, the patrol car in hot pursuit. Fitz exhaled. "At least they didn't stop for us. Let's get out of here." Buffett didn't budge from his lap as he drove to Walmart.

A paw to the face awoke Fitz at 6:00am. "Thanks, Buffett. You sure are a reliable alarm clock. An hour till sunrise, and I need to pee. I guess it'll have to wait. I don't want to use your litter." He rubbed down Buffett's back, eliciting a purr.

"Meow."

"I see. You had ulterior motives for waking me up. It's treat time."

He went through the morning routine of cat treats, heating water for coffee, and eating breakfast. "OK. It's time to go see our park pals. Do you want to go for a walk with Snickers and King?"

"Meow."

He timed it so he would arrive at the park just as the sun began to rise. It was a partly cloudy day, and the sky gradually brightened to a wonderful coral color that spread across the banks of clouds.

Katía's car was already there, but she was nowhere in sight. Fitz's heart sped up. Hopping out of his car he called, "Katía! Katía!"

"Over here by the lake," came a call.

"Good morning. You had me worried," he called back.

"Just trying to do this amazing sunrise justice. I knew it would be spectacular this morning."

Satisfied she was OK, Fitz headed to the bathroom.

The lights of Ben's car came over the hill just as Fitz deposited Buffett's litter into the trash. He was ready with treats when Snickers and King hopped out.

"Surprise," Fitz said, holding out dog biscuits. The dogs gobbled them up eagerly. "Mornin', Ben."

"It's a beautiful one. Where's Katía?"

"She's over by the lake with her camera. It scared me when I first pulled up and she wasn't here."

"Great minds must think alike. Speak of the devil," Ben jutted his chin in the direction from which Katía was approaching.

"I'm not sure that's the right way to speak of a pastor," Fitz laughed.

"It doesn't look like we're ever going to find Zee," Ben moped as Katía joined them.

"Actually, I have the solution. It arrived yesterday," she replied.

Puzzled, Fitz said, "Do you care to explain?"

"I ordered a tracking device. We can use me as a decoy. When they take me to wherever it is they're taking people, you can follow and rescue Zee and me and whomever else they've nabbed."

"No, I don't think so," Ben said. "It's too dangerous."

"It's not any more dangerous than what Zee's facing," Katía protested.

"Have you thought of the things they might do to you?" Fitz asked.

"I have. It's a chance I'm willing to take. I believe Zee is worth it."

"I don't think I'm willing to take that chance," Ben said.

"The first thing they'll do is take your purse and turn off your phone. They'll have your gun. Then they'd find the device which would make them angry. That's not a good recipe," Fitz explained.

"Actually, the device won't be in my purse."

"What if they frisk you?" Ben asked.

"They'd better not be frisking where I'll have the device. Anyway if they find it and turn it off, you'll know to come in a hurry."

An uneasy silence settled over the group. "What makes you think you can just get picked up on demand?" Ben asked. "We have no idea how to find them." More silence.

"I can think of two ways to get her abducted," Fitz stated.

"You're not helping matters," Ben replied.

CHAPTER 26

Max Herringer squirmed in his seat, having difficulty settling in for the long drive to the lab. *Why did I let them talk me into locating it this far away?* He had decided his personal presence might help move the experiments forward. *Just relying on my untrained help certainly isn't working. I'm not sure I can bear to make this drive every day.*

Pulling onto I-85 North from Clairmont Road, he tried to settle into problem solving mode. *I think I understand A6's aphasia, but I don't get A7's nausea and vomiting unless it was the anesthesia. Some people are sensitive to that.*

He pounded his hands on the steering wheel, causing the Mercedes GLE 450 to swerve and elicit a honk from the vehicle in the next lane. "I need to be further along! After seven procedures, Max Herringer should have a cure!" he screamed to the void.

A smile replaced his anger. *Just think of how many actual rats I would have been through by now. I have to remind myself that using expendable human subjects is speeding up the process.* That thought settled his spirit, and he drove on with less agitation.

At 10:18am, Max entered the six-digit code and slipped inside the lab. He hadn't told anyone he was coming today.

The lab was quiet, except for the sound of a soft snore. He rounded the corner and found the lab worker sound asleep on a gurney, the head slightly elevated. Shaking his head in disgust, Max pushed the emergency release, causing the head to crash down and the worker to gasp.

A stream of expletives followed till the worker realized who was standing there. "Hello, Doc. Sorry you caught me snoozing."

"Is that what I'm paying you for?"

"No, sir. But there was nothing to do."

"Nothing to do, huh? Let me make you a list." Max found a sheet of paper and began to list housekeeping duties: clean the toilets, sweep and mop, dust, vacuum the carpet at the entry way. "When you're finished with this, let me know."

Max smiled at the grumbles he heard from the man as he walked away. He didn't bother to ask how the subjects were doing. He would ascertain that himself. He looked over his notes from yesterday, then walked into A6's room.

"Good morning. How are you today?" He did his best to muster some bedside manner. A6 responded with nonsensical speech, stringing words together that didn't fit.

"Let me check the device," Max said, pulling out his scanner. As he reached in to hover the scanner over the deep brain stimulator, A6 punched him in the head. Max's attempt at bedside manner flew out the window, and he punched back. He stormed out of the room to regain control, slamming the door.

"That one's feisty," the lab worker said, passing by with cleaning supplies.

Max didn't respond. He turned his attention to A7. Opening the door, he saw A7 sprawled on the floor in a contorted position, slight foam at his mouth and vomit everywhere. *Looks like a seizure.* "Hey! Get in here!" he called. The lab worker appeared, and Max asked, "How long has he been like this?"

"I don't know. He was in the bed last time I checked."

"And when was that?" Max barked.

"This morning."

Max glared at the worker. "I think you're lying. Cleaning can wait. Dispose of these two first. And this place had better be spotless when I come back."

Settling into the comfort of his Mercedes, Max said, "I guess it's back to the drawing board. What can I do differently?"

Using a burn phone, he called his other helper. "How many do we have in reserve?"

"Just one right now," the voice on the phone answered.

"I need you to get busy. The last two are being terminated." He hung up without waiting for an answer.

CHAPTER 27

Ben sat in the driver's seat of Katía's Prius, arms crossed. "I still think this is a bad idea."

"Unless you can come up with another one, it's the only idea we have," Katía countered from the back seat, craning her neck to see if the Confederate Rising guys had shown.

The Park Pals parked on the street down from the bar the gang members seemed to like. No sign yet. The sound of M&Ms crunching came from the front.

"I see you're nervous, too," Katía said.

"It's not too late to rethink this," Fitz answered.

"Guys, there is something really bad going on, and it's not just that Zee is missing. They are taking homeless folks hostage and doing who knows what to them. The police don't seem to care since they're homeless. Somebody has to do something!"

"You're right," Fitz said. "I would rather be the decoy, though."

"That's chivalrous of you, but I don't think you're their type," she replied.

"True," Fitz agreed.

"They're here," Ben said, alarm registering in his voice.

"Do you have me on your phones?" Katía asked, opening her purse.

"Yes. The signal says you're really close," Ben quipped.

Katía pulled out her Glock and set it on the console between Ben and Fitz. "I don't want them getting their hands on that." She eyed her purse. "Actually, I don't want them getting their grubby hands on this either." She left the purse with them, too.

Fitz kept a check on his watch, giving them ten minutes to make sure they hadn't forgotten something and needed to return to the car. "OK, it's showtime."

Katía got out, pulling out the two stuffed garbage bags she had prepared as part of her homeless person disguise. "Grab these if they make me leave them behind."

"Roger that. Just be careful. And for the record, I still don't like this," Ben said.

"And you be careful with my car," she answered, closing the door. She lugged the two trash bags down the street past the bar door and past the gang's car. *I can't imagine having to carry everything I own with me all the time.*

She stopped and leaned against the building, nerves making every muscle in her body tense. *I won't have to fake having anxiety issues.* Looking down at the bags, she was reminded of the day she ran away from home.

Something had been unfair. What was it? Oh yeah, Mom ordered me to clean the bathroom before I could play. I stormed into my bedroom, stuffed two dolls, their chairs, and a couple of candy bars into my book bag and sneaked out the door. I hid behind one of the apartment buildings, set up my dolls, and ate a candy bar. It seemed like I was there forever. I got bored and decided it would be better to go back home and clean the bathroom. I can't believe she let me just walk out like that. I was only nine.

The bar door opened, and Katía jumped. It was a couple of women who had apparently stopped in for a drink after their shifts at the hospital, judging by their scrub outfits. She took three deep breaths to calm her nerves and went back to waiting.

A cold breeze made the wait even more miserable. She could see the backs of Fitz and Ben's heads. *I imagine they are talking about coming to get me and calling this whole thing off. Maybe that would be best.* While her mind and heart battled with whether to continue, the door to the bar opened, and the four gang members walked out. One burped and they all laughed.

Classy. I guess it's showtime. She eyed the four guys then picked up her bags and started down the street away from them. In her anxious state, she didn't see the rock on the sidewalk. Her ankle turned. She lost her balance and went down. Before she could get up, she saw four pairs of shoes around her.

"Are you OK? Let me help you up," the guy Fitz had identified as the leader said.

Katía started to go along with his offer, then decided it would be better to offer some resistance. "I can manage," she replied, working her way to her feet without letting go of the bags. She tested the ankle. It offered mild soreness but seemed to be OK. "Thanks for the offer, though."

They had her surrounded. "Excuse me," she said and acted as if she were going to continue on her way.

"Please allow us to give you a ride," the leader said.

He can sure act the gentleman. "Thanks, but I like walking."

Taking her arm, he said, "That was an order, not an offer." One of the other guys grabbed the other arm in a vice grip. "And drop those stupid bags," the leader added.

Katía jerked her arms, trying to break free. They held fast. "Leave me alone!" she shouted. *Should I yell for help?*

"If you want to survive, you'll keep your mouth shut and cooperate," one of the guys not holding her arms said, brandishing a knife before quickly tucking it away.

They pushed her into the back seat, one creep getting in on either side of her, both holding knives. *What have I done?* She fought the rising panic. *I have to breathe and stay calm. Fitz and Ben have my back. We have a plan.* She buried her face in her hands and rocked back and forth.

"Stop it, woman. If you cooperate, you have nothing to worry about."

"You're lying," she said. "People don't kidnap a person to do them good."

"That's true. So just be quiet. And be still!"

The car pulled past her Prius. She resisted looking at Fitz and Ben. She resumed her rocking.

"I said stop that," the man to her left said, pushing her back against the seat. "Hurry, Gene. This slut's going to drive me crazy.

The ride seemed like it would never end. They drove out Dawsonville Highway and turned onto Sardis Road. *We're almost at my church. I hope Ben and Fitz are able to find me.*

The car pulled into the driveway of a dark, dilapidated looking house. They dragged Katía out of the car and pulled her toward the front door as darkness took over for the sun.

"Welcome to your vacation home," Gene, the apparent leader, announced. They lifted her onto the little wooden stoop. She noticed the steps had rotted, two lying at odd angles.

"Who gets to frisk her?" one of the guys asked.

Gene backhanded him. "Shut up. We're outside." He unlocked the door and they shoved her inside.

Something about stepping through that doorway set off Katía's fear. It seemed so final. She started fighting to get out, but they held her fast. She kicked one in the knee, and he punched her in the stomach. A groan erupted from her mouth, and she doubled over.

Gene backhanded that one, too. "Idiot! You know the boss doesn't want his rats to be harmed."

"She kicked me in the knee."

"You're saying a girl hurt you?"

The guy shut up. The flashlights on two of their phones broke the darkness. Katía shielded her eyes as they shined right at her.

"Moe, you do the honors." He was the only one left who hadn't been backhanded.

"Gladly," Moe answered.

Katía jumped when Moe's hands hit her waist, sliding slowly along. He moved down one leg and up the other, lingering at her crotch. Sliding up her buttocks, he moved to between her breasts, then underneath them.

"What is that? She's got something in there!" Moe said, sounding frightened.

"You want Moe to pull it out, or would you rather do it yourself?" Gene asked.

She wanted to run, to escape, to be back home where she felt safe. She was paralyzed. *Why did I ever think I could do this?*

"Suit yourself," Gene said. "Moe will be happy to fish it out.

The thought of Moe groping around in her bra scared her into action. She reached under her shirt and pulled out the tracking device. "There." She handed it over.

"What is it?" Moe asked.

Gene lit up the flashlight on his phone and studied the little object. "I ain't never seen anything like it, but it can't be good. What have you done?" He found the power button and turned it off. "What is this thing?" he shouted, getting nose to nose with her.

"It's my pedometer. It tells me how many steps I take each day."

"You don't think I can smell a lie? It's probably some kind of tracking device. We have to get out of here! Get her and the other prisoner into the car now!"

"But we don't have room for both of them," one of the others said.

"This one can ride in the trunk, Ernie," Gene sneered.

Ernie and Moe picked up Katía. She lost her cool and began kicking and screaming.

"Pop the trunk," Ernie called as they hopped off the stoop.

Katía's back crashed onto several hard items. The crash of the trunk lid left her in total darkness. She heard the doors slam, and the car began to move, each bump sending shockwaves through her back. *I have to get out of here. And I have to get off whatever I'm lying on.*

CHAPTER 28

Fitz kept a laser focus on his phone, calling out directions as Ben drove. They were following about a mile behind the dot on the screen.

"Taking a right onto Sardis Road," Fitz announced as they approached the bridge over Lake Lanier, passing the marina on the left. He tried relaxing his grip on the phone. He already had one hand braced on his leg to stop the bouncing. "I don't like this. I wish we hadn't let her go through with it."

"Now you realize it's a bad idea. I tried to tell you two. I wish Luna hadn't been out of town. She would have nixed the idea."

"They're turning left onto Fran Mar Drive." He looked up and stretched his neck, not having moved his eyes from the phone since they started following. "There are some rundown places in there."

When he looked back down, the dot had stopped moving. He waited a few seconds before saying, "I think we have the location." He felt the car accelerate.

Looking over, he noticed Ben had a death grip on the steering wheel. "Slow down. I think we need to give them time to get her locked up. Then they will probably leave, if it's like the first house."

"What if this is where the gang stays? Did you think of that?" Ben was getting testy.

"I did. Last time they had an abandoned house with no power. I don't believe these guys are into roughing it like that."

"I hope you're right."

"You didn't slow down," Fitz noted.

Ben muttered something as he pulled into the lane to turn right onto Sardis.

"There's a church across from where you turn onto Fran Mar. Let's park there for a bit and see what happens," Fitz directed.

"I say we go on and get her."

"We would be risking the chance of a gun battle. Who knows what would happen. Patience is the better option."

Ben muttered again but turned right to enter the church parking lot, pointing the car so they could see the road. Ben whipped out his phone and stared at the dot.

Two gasps signaled the moment the tracker turned off. Fitz and Ben looked at each other, the phones shining an eerie light in the darkness.

"What happened?" Ben asked.

"They found the tracker."

Ben cranked the car. "We have to go."

"Wait. It's still better to be patient. They will be expecting someone now. They'll be on high alert. Let's give them a minute to settle down and decide that maybe she wasn't being followed."

Ben muttered again, cutting off the car. "You're going to give me a heart attack."

Fitz checked his watch, and a tense silence pressed in, both men staring at their phones.

"Twenty minutes," Fitz said while memorizing the last location of the tracker's signal.

"I hope they're not retaliating for her having the tracker," Ben said.

They sat in the darkness, each minute seeming longer than the previous one. The shine of car lights dragged them from their phone screens.

"That's the Charger," Ben croaked, his voice tense from the strain of waiting.

"They left quicker than I thought they would," Fitz observed. Ben had already cranked the car. "Let them get on ahead before you move. We don't want to draw their attention."

With the Charger out of sight, Ben tore out of the parking lot.

"Slow down. It's coming up. The next driveway."

Ben turned in, and the car lights revealed a dilapidated white frame house. No lights shone from the windows. "I have a bad feeling about this."

Fitz had been having the same feeling ever since the guys left earlier than he expected. He didn't voice his concern because he didn't want to upset Ben more. *It's going to be empty.*

With the Beretta in hand, Fitz led Ben toward the house. Fitz paused at the door, listening. Nothing. He tried the door knob. It was unlocked. He turned on the flashlight on his phone and signaled for Ben to open the door.

Fitz rushed in, scanning the room. He proceeded room by room. It was a two bed, one bathroom house, and it was empty except for two twin beds. Returning to the den, he found Ben holding the smashed tracker.

"We lost her," Ben sighed.

Fitz's mind was racing too hard to respond, trying to determine their next step. He noticed Ben had his phone to his ear. "What are you doing?"

"I need to report an abduction," Ben spoke into his phone. "Ben Blessing… Katía Bancroft… I don't know the address… OK, I won't turn it off."

"What were you thinking?" Fitz asked, tugging on his beard. "They will probably arrest us for putting her in danger."

"We need help finding her. This is out of control and beyond our ability to manage," Ben growled.

It was Fitz's turn to mutter expletives under his breath. He walked in circles. *We should run. They will have located the house by now. All we have to do is turn off Ben's phone and go.* "Turn off your phone and let's get out of here. I don't want to be arrested."

"They're not going to arrest us, and we have no way to find her. We screwed up, Fitz! This is our fault! They might kill her! I can't believe you! Don't you care what happens to her?" Ben was shouting by the end.

His accusation hit Fitz hard. It hurt. *Why do people always say that? I do care. I care a lot.* His mind flashed back to a time he had shared with Sharon on Matapang Beach in Guam. They drank beer in chairs under umbrellas, holding hands as they watched the waves crash. Snorkeling in the morning and making love in the evenings had made it the best three days of his life. *I had been so tempted to ask her to marry me. We could have retired from the military and built a life together. It was the last time I saw her.* Fitz's heart was breaking all over again. His memory was beginning to lose the details of her smile, her eyes, the curls of her black hair. *I'm grateful for the photos I have. They help refresh this old memory.*

The sound of a siren pulled him from his thoughts. *Where am I?* He hadn't realized that he'd walked out of the house and down the street during his retreat into the past. *Maybe it's for the best.*

CHAPTER 29

Every bump drove home the discomfort in Katía's back as well as the realization that she was in a predicament. She dug the hard objects from under her to get more comfortable. They felt like pieces of wood.

Lord, I may have done something stupid. I don't know if you have an answer for stupid, but I need your help. I was trying to help find Zee, and now look at the situation I'm in. Please help me get out of this. And help us find Zee, too. Thanks. Amen.

Opening her eyes after the prayer, she noticed a faint glow above her. *What is that?* Being the driver of a hatchback, she wasn't aware of the emergency release inside a trunk.

The faint light distracted her from her danger. Studying the yellow glow, she decided it must be a release lever. Hope grew. *Thanks, Lord. When the car stops, I can pop the trunk, jump out, and run. Maybe they don't know it's here.* She reached and touched the lever, feeling safer now that she had a plan.

The car slowed, and Katía readied herself. It came to a stop, but just as she reached for the lever, it began to move again. *Patience. They say that's a virtue. Lord, help me to know when it's time.* From the road noise, she could tell the car was moving fast.

She thought about her cats, two identical white long-haired kitties named Snow and Cotton. *Y'all will be OK. I left food and water. The litter might get stinky, though. I'm glad it has an automatic scooper.*

A memory from childhood popped into her mind. Cranks was a cat she had as a child. She and her mom named him Cranks because he could be cranky at times. *He would jump up onto the table and then on top of the privacy fence on the little patio behind our apartment. I was always afraid he would run away, but he never did. Mom always said he knew he had it good with us.*

Katía had grown up in a bad neighborhood. She was familiar with guys like the ones driving the car. She had seen terrible things happen, including a knife fight in the parking lot outside her apartment. That was the main reason her mom insisted on having a gun and on Katía's knowing how to use it.

I wish I had the gun now. I wonder if this is where my life ends. No, I can't think like that. I'm going to get out of this. I need to focus on the plan. I think it will be best to run to the driver's side. There will only be one after me on that side. The others will have to run around the car first, and I doubt the driver will abandon the car. I will have to watch for traffic. They did say the boss wanted me unharmed, so hopefully they won't shoot.

As she planned her escape, a feeling began to surface. It grew into a prompting in her heart then emerged as a thought. *What do you mean I shouldn't try to escape, Lord? I need to get away from these maniacs.*

She listened and the feeling persisted. *Is that really you telling me to do this?* She listened to her heart, trying to discern if this idea was craziness or God leading her. Whatever it was warmed her heart and became stronger. *OK, God, but you had better have my back like you had Daniel's in the lion's den.* An odd nervous joy followed her little prayer. *I can't believe I'm going to just let them take me wherever.*

The car came to a stop, and she heard the doors open. "Get this one in first," she heard Gene say.

"What about the one in the trunk? We should do something special to her," Ernie suggested.

"Shut up. Our payment depends on them being delivered in good shape, fool," Gene reprimanded.

I hope they stick to that. Silence followed, and she found herself straining to hear something, anything. The emptiness stretched on. *I wonder if they're inside.* Her nerves began to fray. *Should I try to get out?* The temptation to pull the release lever grew with each breath.

"Ready?" Gene's voice startled her. He was right behind the car. The trunk popped open, and all four of the thugs stood, looking ready for a fight. Gene held a pistol.

"Get out," he ordered.

Katía knew there was no chance of resisting. She dragged herself out of the trunk, nerves on high alert. Moe and Ernie each grabbed an arm and pulled her to a door.

Taking note of her surroundings, she saw they were leading her into a building. *A small warehouse? Shop? No security lights? No windows? What kind of place is this?*

CHAPTER 30

itz looked back at the flashing blue lights in the driveway of the abandoned house and decided he was in no mood to deal with a deputy. He kept walking. *What have we done? Maybe Ben was right to call it in. But they haven't bothered to arrest those guys yet. I guess they could have questioned them and let them go. The creeps are probably good liars.*

Anger began to build. *This should never have gotten this far. Those four should have been apprehended days ago. It's not like they're trying to hide. Something's not right here.*

Fitz was so deep in thought that he hadn't noticed a car had pulled beside him. The window rolled down, and Ben asked, "Where are you going?"

"I have no idea."

"Want a ride?"

Fitz was so mad he didn't want to get into the car. "No, I'm good."

"It's a long way to your car, and Uber would be expensive."

Fitz got even angrier knowing Ben was right. The best option was to get into the car. He walked a few more steps just for spite. "Fine. I'll get in."

"It was your good buddy, Ron, who responded to the call. Maybe it was best that you walked away." Fitz tapped his foot on the floorboard.

"He said he would alert all of the deputies and Gainesville City officers to be on the lookout for the Charger and to apprehend them when they find them. He's even passing it on to the State Patrol. I think they're finally taking this seriously. Look what I found," he said, holding up a dog biscuit.

Fitz continued tapping his foot. His mind was trying to predict where they might have taken Katía. *They turned right onto Sardis Road, so they're headed back into town. This is the second house they've abandoned. Could they have a third? Would they go back to the first one, hoping no one would come back there? Could we find a list of abandoned houses in the area? Would it be a waste of time to go by that first house? We don't have time to waste.*

Sound filtered into Fitz's consciousness. Ben was talking. "Anybody home over there?"

"I was thinking. What is it?"

"You didn't hear a word I said, did you?"

"No."

"Pay attention. I found a dog biscuit in one of the rooms while I was waiting. Zee was there."

"He was? So they're together now?" Fitz responded.

"What are the chances they would go back to the first house?"

"I was wondering that, too. I don't think they would. They should think that is the first place we would look. We need a computer, and the library is closed."

"What do we need a computer for?" Ben asked.

"We might be able to identify unoccupied homes in the county." A new thought crossed his mind, bringing hope for the first time. "With a little luck, we might even be able to find where these goats live."

"We can use our phones instead of a computer, but how could we find where they live?" Ben wondered.

"I'm going to try calling in a favor. Do you still have the picture of their tag?"

"Of course."

"Let me see it."

"I can't open the phone while I'm driving."

"Well pull over then." Fitz realized he was getting testy. He popped some M&Ms into his mouth to help calm down.

Pulling into a church parking lot, Ben handed Fitz his phone with the photo pulled up. Fitz placed a call to the Hall County Sheriff's Department.

"Is Geraldine on tonight… Hey, Geraldine, it's Fitz… I'm in a pickle and need some help… Would you please run a tag number and give me a name and address? It would be the one Ron called in the BOLO on…"

A surge of anger hit like a hammer. Fitz couldn't speak. *He hasn't called it in?* He heard Geraldine calling his name. "Sorry. Are you sure he hasn't called in a BOLO on an orange Dodge Charger? A friend of mine just called in an abduction a few minutes ago. He gave him the tag number… I see. Would you mind issuing the BOLO?… Come on, Geraldine! A Black pastor has been kidnapped by a gang of white supremacists. It's not going to turn out well if we don't do something now!" *I'm shouting. I shouldn't shout.*

"Can you run the tag number and give me the address… I see. Well at least call Ron and ask him about it… Thanks." He disconnected, not believing what he had just heard. "Ron didn't issue the BOLO," he told Ben.

"Why not?"

Fitz sat silently except for the tapping of his foot, his mind racing. "Why would he do that?" He was talking to himself. "The policy is that the BOLO be issued immediately not after the report is written. He's a sorry guy, but I didn't think he was that low. I'm calling Geraldine back.

"Geraldine, please… It's Fitz again. Do you have any reports from Ron on recent abductions?… I see. Thanks."

Fitz disconnected and turned to Ben. "He hasn't written up reports on any of the abductions."

"What?"

"He is in on whatever is happening. We're not going to get any help from law enforcement."

"Couldn't Geraldine issue one?"

"She has to have the request from a deputy or other law enforcement official. She can't take it from me."

"We've lost her, and there's no telling what they will do."

Fitz could hear the angst in Ben's voice. *I have to come up with a plan. Options. I need options.* Another handful of M&Ms. "I see two options. We could drive around hoping we run into them or look up unoccupied houses and check them out. I think the latter has more chance of success. And we need food and coffee."

Ben raced out of the parking lot. "There's a Wendy's on the way to my house. We can do that kind of search better on a computer."

Fitz wolfed down his burger while Ben booted up the laptop.

"I have no idea where to start," Ben said.

"Just do a search for unoccupied houses in Hall County, Georgia." He leaned in over Ben's shoulder. "I think our best bet is to search the foreclosed properties under HUD."

Ben pulled up the site.

"Holy buzzard beaks! There are over seven hundred properties. We have to narrow that down somehow. We are definitely going to need coffee," Fitz moaned. He looked over, and Ben had his head cocked. "What?"

"You have an odd way of cussing," Ben noted.

"Mom dressed me down for cussing one day when I was a kid. It stuck, and I had to come up with an alternative."

"Interesting. I'll make the coffee."

Fitz turned back to the computer. *How are we going to narrow down this list?* "You don't have another computer, do you?"

"No, but I have a phone."

"Pull up this site and start going through the pictures looking for potential houses they might use. We know their style, white and dumpy. I think we can eliminate any nice looking houses."

Fitz skipped to the middle and began clicking through. "Hey, I need a pen and paper."

"Great minds think alike," Ben said, laying pen and paper on the table just as Fitz asked. They set to scanning the homes.

"I have a feeling this is it," Fitz said after finding a dilapidated white frame house. He finished working through the houses. "I've got fifteen possibilities."

"Twelve for me," Ben replied. "That's twenty-seven to visit."

"We'll need coffee to go."

"We also need to map out this quest so we're not ping ponging around the county."

Fitz just wanted to get up and go to that one house he had the hunch over. "Look at this place," he pulled up the house. "Let's head there, and I'll work on entering the addresses into the mapping app while you drive."

Ben poured up two thermoses of coffee, and they hit the car. Fitz noticed hesitation about being in the car that long was missing. *I guess finding Katia is more important than my anxiety.*

CHAPTER 31

Fitz struggled to enter addresses into the app while the car was moving. He was still at it when Ben pulled into the driveway of the house he had had the hunch about. The house was dark as he had expected.

"This could be dangerous. You should stay in the car," Fitz suggested.

"Oh, please. Nobody's staying in the car. Let's go before they have time to run out the back." Ben opened the door and got out. Fitz followed, Beretta in hand.

They hurried onto the stoop. "Should we knock?" Ben asked.

Fitz shook his head and tried the door. "Locked," he whispered.

"I'm not surprised."

Fitz put a finger to his lips and pointed to the back. He left the stoop and rounded the corner of the house. When he reached the back corner, he heard a low "Woof." In the darkness he could just make out a large black dog. *It must be chained.*

Another low "Woof."

"You first," Ben whispered from behind.

"I think I'll go back to the front door. Maybe I can open it." Car lights turning into the driveway drew their attention. "Looks like we have company."

Creeping back to the corner of the house, Fitz peeked around to see a man getting out of a pickup truck. "I think he has a shotgun."

The man walked to the front door and tested it. "Gentleman, I don't take kindly to intruders. Come on out, and we can settle this peacefully," he called.

Fitz slid the Beretta back into its holster and made sure his coat covered it. "Coming out," he called and walked forward holding his hands up. Ben followed.

"Care to explain yourselves?" the man asked.

"We have reason to believe that gang members might be holding hostages in your home," Fitz explained.

The man laughed. "Is that the best you can come up with?"

"Actually, it's the truth," Ben said. "A gang named Confederate Rising has been abducting Black people. They have been holding them in abandoned houses like this one. They have two of our friends, and we're trying to find them."

The man lowered the shotgun but still held it with two hands. "I have surveillance. I would have known had someone broken in, just like I knew you were prowling around."

"Do you mind checking, just to make sure?" Ben asked.

"Good grief," he grumped as he fished keys from his pocket.

Ben and Fitz started for the stoop. "Nope. You wait right there," the man said, raising the shotgun again. He disappeared inside the house, then returned. "No signs of any prisoners. Now will you kindly get off my property? It's still mine till the bank files the papers tomorrow."

Back in the car, Ben waited for the pickup truck to pull out before he could back up. "That's one down. I hope we have better luck at the next one."

Fitz opened his phone and tapped the start button for directions to the next house. He checked his watch: 9:49. *I checked Buffett's food. He's OK. Ben let the dogs out. I guess we're good for the night.* He sipped on the coffee. *Where have they taken you?*

Fitz could see lights on as they approached the next house. "Drive by then turn around. The lights are on. That's different."

"We might as well stop since we're here," Ben said as he pulled into the third driveway down. When he got back and turned into the driveway of the house they were looking for, they could see a woman carrying a box through the living room.

"Looks like they're moving out. Let's try the next house," Fitz noted.

Ben pulled into the driveway of the third house on their list. The headlights revealed peeling paint and a partially caved in roof on the front porch. "Five star resort," he quipped.

"Maybe the third time's a charm," Fitz hoped. "No sign of the Charger."

They hopped out and hurried to the front door. The second step collapsed under Fitz's weight. Ben steadied him. "I think this might be below even their standards," Ben said.

Fitz heard movement inside. "Someone's here," he whispered. He tested each step, proceeding as quietly as he could on the creaky wood. A curtain moved in the front window, freezing Fitz in his tracks. Holding the Beretta behind his back, he moved to the door and knocked.

Silence. He knocked again. "I know you're in there. We're looking for friends of ours."

Finally, feet shuffled to the door, and it opened a crack. "We're looking for a Black man and woman who've been abducted," Fitz explained.

"I ain't seen 'em," the toothless African American man answered.

"Do you mind if we look to make sure they're not here?" Fitz asked calmly while sliding his toe into the crack.

"This is my place. Go away."

"We'll leave you be as soon as we've had a look around." Fitz's patience was crumbling.

The man tried to push the door closed, but Fitz's shoe blocked it. He rammed his shoulder into the door, knocking the man backwards. Ben's flashlight came on at the same time Fitz brought his gun around.

Fear flashed in the man's eyes. He raised his hands. "I just needed a place to stay. I didn't hurt nothin'."

"It's OK," Ben soothed. "We just need to see if our friends are here. You don't have to leave."

Fitz was moving quickly from room to room. "You the only one here?" he asked.

"Yeah."

Fitz's shoulders slumped. *The third time wasn't a charm. It was another dead end.* He started to walk out. "Hold this." He handed the gun to Ben and pulled out his wallet. Handing the man a twenty dollar bill, he said, "Sorry for the trouble."

Fitz's heart sank as his bottom sank into the seat of Ben's car. "I don't think we're going to find them."

"We have to keep trying. You know they took them somewhere."

Fitz started the directions to the next house on the map. "At least we're doing something instead of sitting around worrying."

"I'm open to a better idea if you have one. Otherwise let's stick with this plan."

"What if we look all night and don't find them? They could be sold into whatever they were abducted for by then. I can't believe we let Katía do that."

"I wasn't for it to start with."

Fitz didn't respond. Ben's comment added a hundred pounds to the weight of the guilt pressing into his chest.

CHAPTER 32

atía's heart raced as Moe and Ernie pushed her through the door. Her eyes adjusted to the lights shining in a small reception area. They dragged her around the desk and through another door.

This led into a hall with several doors. She glanced into the first room. *Is that an operating table?* Fear flooded her heart. *What are they going to do to me?* She saw gurneys in two other rooms. They pushed her through the door at the end of the hall.

"Sit down!" Ernie ordered.

Katía wanted to run. Her heart told her to fight, but her mind said there was no chance. She would have to overpower four men, and the last one had a gun. She forced herself to sit on the bed.

"Your arm, please." A sickening grin formed on Ernie's face. He ran his hand up her arm toward her shoulder. "Yum. Soft."

She couldn't stand it and jerked away.

"Get on with it," Moe said.

They're going to rape me.

Ernie turned an angry glare toward Moe then snatched Katía's leg. "Can't a guy enjoy the merchandise?" He slapped a handcuff around her ankle.

"Not unless you want to deal with Gene," Moe answered.

Without another word, they left the room. It was dark except for the light shining in from the hallway. Katía felt the cuff and discovered it was attached to a chain that was attached to the bed frame. *I could disassemble the bed and get away.*

"You gonna call and tell him what happened?" floated down the hallway.

"Have you lost your mind? What he doesn't know can't hurt us. Let's find a new place to keep them," Gene answered.

She waited, hope coursing through her veins. When she heard the door at the end of the hall close, she searched the walls for a light switch. *That's odd.* She kept feeling her way around, up and down. She never found a switch.

Going back to the bed, she got down on her knees and felt around. The mattress was on top of a sheet of plywood that rested on a metal frame. *This is the kind of frame that comes apart in the middle and folds.*

She listened but heard no signs of her captors. Lifting the mattress, she slid it to the side. Next she moved the plywood. Feeling along the frame, she located the spot in the center where it came apart. She pushed to unlatch it, but the pieces didn't move. She pushed harder. Nothing.

She felt along the frame and found that it had been bolted together. She tried to twist the nut, but it wouldn't budge. *Of course they thought of that.* Hope dashed away, and she hung her head. Then a thought sent a shock through her. *I can carry this little bed frame!*

Standing, she grabbed the edge and pulled. The light weight frame didn't budge. It was bolted to the floor. Just as quickly, her hope was crushed again. She put the plywood and mattress back onto the frame and sat down.

Head in her hands, tears began to flow. *Lord, I need your help. We need your help. I don't know what they have planned, but it can't be good.*

She heard footsteps in the hall and froze, holding her breath as if silence could make her disappear. A door opened and closed. She ventured to open her eyes and look into the hallway. It was just as it had been. A toilet flushed and the door she had heard before opened again.

"Is anybody else here?" a man called.

"Zee? Is that you?" Katía asked.

"Katía?"

Katía flew to the hallway and grabbed Zee in a hug, tears resuming their flow.

"What are you doing here?" Zee asked.

Wiping the tears from her cheeks, she began. "We were trying to find you. The police wouldn't help since you're homeless. We decided to try getting me kidnapped while I was wearing a tracking device, hoping it would lead to you."

"That's the dumbest thing I ever heard of! Are you crazy? You shouldn't have done that."

"Well, it worked… sort of."

"What do you mean, 'sort of?'"

"I found you, but they found the tracking device. Now Fitz and Ben don't know where we are."

Zee put his hands on his hips and hung his head. "I wish you hadn't risked yourself for me. You don't deserve this kind of treatment."

"You don't either, Zee. What have they done to you?"

"I've just been chained to a bed in an empty house, living on granola bars and water."

"We found the dog biscuit you left at the first house."

"I was hoping someone would find that."

"What do you think the plan is? I'm sure they're planning more than chaining us to beds."

"I don't know. They haven't told me. The only thing I've heard is that their boss needs us healthy. I assume we're to be sold into some kind of slavery. I don't think I'd be much of a catch for sex trafficking," he chuckled.

Katía started to ask Zee if he had seen the operating table but decided it might frighten him. *Best not to add another thing to worry about.*

"The bathroom is in there," Zee said, pointing to the door. We have just enough leash to reach the toilet. They're generous that way. I found granola bars and water on the floor. I'm getting tired of granola bars. I'd sure like a burger and fries."

"Is anyone else here?"

"I haven't heard anyone. There wasn't a greeting committee."

"Hey! Is anyone here?" Katía shouted. Zee jumped. Silence was the only response.

CHAPTER 33

It was 3:04am. Ben drove into the darkness toward their ninth house. He tipped his thermos up for the fourth time since he had finished it. "The coffee's gone."

Ben's comment prompted Fitz to take a sip of his. "Mine's cold." He was getting frustrated. Frustrated and anxious. The M&Ms weren't helping much. He popped a few more into his mouth anyway. He had quit counting out three at a time.

"We're not going to find her," Fitz muttered to himself.

"What's that?" Ben asked.

"Nothing. I was talking to myself." The long time in Ben's car was wearing on Fitz's nerves almost as much as losing Katía.

"We're not going to find her, are we?" Ben stated.

"It's not looking good."

"What are we going to do?"

The worry in Ben's voice matched Fitz's own state of angst. *It would be easy for us to spiral into panic. We have to stay calm and focus.* "I don't know." He recognized a hollow, hopeless sound in his own voice.

Ben pulled into the driveway of their next target. Like so many times that night, the front door was locked, so they went around back. A window in the back door was broken out and the door stood partly open.

"Hello! Anyone here?" Fitz called. No answer. He pushed through the door and turned on the flashlight app.

He and Ben separated and checked out all the rooms.

"Anything?" Ben asked.

"Nope. Empty just like the last seven. This is pointless." The disappointment stung.

"They have to have taken them somewhere."

Fitz hammered his hand onto the wall, his fist crashing through the sheetrock.

"Feel better?" Ben asked.

"No."

"Let's get moving to number ten then."

Fitz walked to the car without a response. As Ben backed out of the driveway, Fitz said, "I think we need another plan. Food and another plan." *I'm out of M&Ms.* He searched his mind for options in the area.

"I need gas, too."

They were in the small town of Lula. "There's a gas station and Waffle House on the expressway. Take a left at the four-way stop."

While Ben pumped the gas, Fitz went in and restocked his M&Ms. They crossed Highway 365 and pulled into the Waffle House. Fitz ordered eggs and pancakes. Ben had eggs and hashbrowns.

"What could we do differently?" Fitz asked. *That was always the question I'd ask myself during an investigation.*

"We could split up and cover more houses," Ben suggested.

"I wish we'd thought of that before we started. I think we need a different approach."

"I don't want to wait that long, but we could sit outside the bar tomorrow… oops, I mean this afternoon." Ben took a gulp of the orange juice the waitress just deposited onto the table.

"We'll definitely do that if we haven't found them before. What else could we do now?" Fitz blew on his coffee before taking a sip. *My brain's tired. I'm too old to try to function all night.*

"Back in your police days, how would you find someone?"

"First of all, I'd issue a BOLO and get other officers involved. Second, I'd look up the address associated with the car and go there. If that didn't work, I'd have surveillance mining the traffic camera footage for the car." Fitz tried to mine his mind while he buttered his pancakes. "You worked in computers. Do you have any ideas?"

Ben swallowed a bite of hashbrowns, then smiled. "I'll probably regret this, but I might be able to get into the traffic camera system."

"What do you mean?"

"You know I worked in computers. I had a side gig of hacking into systems to help companies identify vulnerabilities."

"You can do that?" Fitz was surprised.

"Yeah. I can do that."

They were almost finished with their food when Fitz jumped up. "Come on!" He took three steps toward the door, then tore his wallet out of his pocket and threw two twenties on the table.

"What's the rush?"

"The Charger's at the stoplight!"

They flew out the door. The light turned green, and the Charger turned onto Highway 365.

"Hurry!" Fitz urged.

"I'm moving as fast as an old man can," Ben replied.

* * * * *

Gene checked his watch as he and the other three got out of the car: 3:04am. "Let's get this trash to the new house and go to bed. The slut gets the trunk again."

Moe and Boomer loaded Zee into the back seat while Gene and Ernie forced Katía into the trunk.

"Want me to ride back here with you? We could get real close," Ernie taunted.

"Shut up and get in," Gene said, closing the trunk. He slid into the driver's seat and took off.

"Hurry up. I'm getting sleepy," Boomer commented.

"You're always the lazy one," Gene replied.

"I can't help it if I need my beauty sleep," Boomer answered.

"Don't you think it's time to let us go?" Zee asked from the back seat where he was wedged in between Moe and Boomer.

"I didn't hear anyone say you could talk," Moe said, elbowing Zee in the ribs.

"At least let the woman go. What kind of men would make a woman ride in the trunk. You can't be proud of yourselves."

Another jab drew a grunt from Zee. Gene listened to the comment with disdain. "How dare you question our integrity!" Gene snapped. "You're lower than dirt. It really doesn't matter what we do with you."

Moe responded with another jab in the ribs.

"Enough, Moe. If you break a rib, the boss might not pay us." Gene drove on in silence, heading toward Lula. *I shouldn't even have to listen to him talk. We are such a superior race. He is nothing, just a bug to be smashed under my foot.* Anger roiled his gut as he thought about Black people claiming to be equal to him. He realized he had a death grip on the steering wheel. *There's no need for me to get worked up about it. I might do something I'd regret… moneywise, that is.*

He pulled into the driveway of a rundown house. Falling siding glared in the car lights. "See what we need to do to get in," Gene ordered.

Ernie hopped out and tried the front door. Gene watched as he hurried around the side. In a few seconds, the front door opened.

"If you know what's good for you, you'll keep quiet," he directed Zee in a threatening voice. "Get him set up, then we'll deal with what's in the back."

"If you're good, we'll give you enough line to reach the slut," Boomer added.

"Shut up, Boomer," Gene demanded. "Take him in." As the night wore on, the testier he felt. He wanted to get home where it was warm and go to sleep.

As Moe and Boomer dragged Zee into the house, Ernie returned to the car.

"Pop the trunk," Gene ordered. Gun drawn, he growled, "If you say a word, it'll be your last. Get out."

Katía crawled out of the trunk, and Gene and Ernie dragged her into the house.

"What are you going to do with us?" Katía asked.

Gene nearly backhanded her but stopped just in time. "It really doesn't matter, does it. You are under my control, and I'll do whatever I want."

Ernie shackled Katía, then said, "We could teach her a lesson before we go."

This time Gene didn't hold back. He backhanded Ernie. "How many times do I have to tell you?" Gene turned and walked through the house, pausing to notice a hole in the sheet rock.

CHAPTER 34

Ben pulled out of the Waffle House parking lot and turned right onto Highway 365, heading south toward Gainesville.

"You have to go fast enough to catch up," Fitz urged, wishing he were driving. He leaned forward, trying to will the car to go faster.

"I'm up to seventy-five," Ben complained. He started to slow down.

"What are you doing? I think that's them up ahead!" Fitz complained before noticing the blue flash illuminating the car. "Oh."

Ben continued to slow and veered onto the shoulder. "A ticket is just what I need."

Fitz held his breath. The police car passed by. "Maybe they're after the Charger."

Ben pulled back into the lane, driving just fast enough not to gain on the blue lights ahead. They watched as the police car turned right onto Ramsey Road.

"Do we follow the officer or stay on three sixty-five?" Ben asked.

Fitz strained to see ahead. "I don't see anything ahead. Follow the blue lights."

Ben hit the brakes and made the turn. They followed as the officer turned right onto White Sulphur Road. Just as they neared the traffic light, the lights and siren from an ambulance appeared, coming from the other direction.

Fitz slammed his hand onto his knee. "We lost them!" He hadn't felt so low since he was fired. *Katía was depending on me, and I failed her.*

"What do you think they'll do to her?" Ben whispered.

"I have no idea." Fitz could hear the dejection in Ben's voice. *I really am worthless, just like Ron said on the day I left the sheriff's office.* He remembered the new bag of M&Ms and pulled them open, popping three into his mouth. *I have to regain my balance. Falling into anxiety will not help Katía or Zee. What's the next step? I have to find the next step.*

"I say we go back to the house and try some computer work," Ben suggested.

"Sounds good." Fitz was relieved that Ben saw a way forward. *I just hope it works.*

✳ ✳ ✳ ✳ ✳

Katía pulled with all her might on the chain, fear and frustration propelling her. It didn't budge. She felt and found they had screwed two-by-fours to the wall and had the chain run through it. *That's probably what I was lying on in the trunk. I should be able to break that.* She jerked again, succeeding only in hurting her hands.

"Zee? Are you here?"

"Yes, ma'am."

"Can you break the chain free?"

"I doubt it, but I'll try." She heard the sound of the chain being tugged and Zee grunting. "Nope. It looks like they knew what they were doing."

Katía's heart sank as she walked into the hallway. "We have to get out of here." Zee met her there. She could hear him running his hand along the wall. A light switch flicked.

"Nope. No electricity," he said.

"We don't even have beds this time. And it's cold."

"You can have my coat."

She heard Zee's coat unzipping. "No, but thanks, Zee. That's gallant of you, but we need to keep both of us alive."

"I wonder if they'll be back tonight."

"I hope not. They give me the creeps."

"I'm sure Fitz and Ben are still looking. Maybe they'll find us soon," Zee offered.

Katía realized Zee was trying to give her hope. "Thanks, Zee. I hope so, too. In the meantime, we need to look around and see if we can find a tool to help us escape. I wonder if they got the boards they screwed to the walls from here?"

"I got to hold them while we drove up here."

"I think I may have been lying on them while they drove us to that building. How many handcuffs can they have?" Katía wondered.

"Seems like an endless supply. Maybe they robbed the police."

"Let's get to hunting." Katía tested the length of her chain. It went all the way to the kitchen. She flung open drawers and cabinets, feeling through each for a potential tool that might free them.

Zee joined her and looked through the pantry. "Nothin' here but empty shelves."

"Somebody cleaned this house up way too much. It must have been the owner getting ready to sell it."

"Could've been the bank foreclosed on it and had someone clean it out."

"Either way, all we have is empty drawers. We could use them to hit the jerks over the head the next time they show up," Katía said, wondering if that would actually work.

"If my math is right, there are four of them, and one of them has a gun. Besides, it would be obvious we're holding drawers when they walk in."

"You sure know how to ruin a gal's plans."

"Sorry," Zee replied. "Just trying to stay alive."

"Have they told you what they plan to do to us?" A shudder went through Katía's body when she asked that.

"Not that I remember. I'm not even sure how long I've been a prisoner."

"It's been a week, Zee."

"No wonder I'm sick of granola bars."

"Why didn't I think of this before?" Katía started toward the front door, but the chain stopped her.

"Think of what?"

"Yelling for help." She moved to the window in the room where her chain was attached. "You might want to cover your ears." Opening the window, she yelled for help till she started getting hoarse.

The window looked out the back, so she couldn't see any other houses. She waited, hoping to hear a knock at the door, someone asking if they were OK.

She went and found Zee sitting in the hall. "That ought to get somebody's attention," he said.

Sitting down beside him she tried to muster some hope. *Lord, please let my call rouse someone with a caring heart. Amen.*

Zee's head slid onto her shoulder, his breathing slow and steady.

CHAPTER 35

Getting out of the car, Fitz made a bee line to check on Buffett. He hopped into the driver's seat. "How ya doing, Buddy?"

Buffett stretched, then hopped into his lap and purred. Fitz stroked his back. "I've got more work to do if we're going to find Zee and Katía. You be a good cat." As he made a move to get out, Buffett jumped into the back seat.

"Wait. It's cold. Let me see what I can do." He headed for the house. "Hey, Ben, would you mind if Buffett slept in your garage? It's cold. I'll bring the litter."

"No way. Bring him into the house and we'll put him in the spare bedroom so the dogs won't bother him."

"Thanks." Fitz and Ben went about setting the cat up like royalty, which of course, Buffett considered himself to be.

"This is going to take a while, so make yourself at home. I put on more coffee, or you can have a nap," Ben said.

A thought struck Fitz. *Should I ask? He did say to make myself at home. It would feel so good, and it's been so long.* He hesitated but finally couldn't resist asking. "Would you mind if I had a shower?"

A surprised look formed on Ben's face followed by recognition. "No, of course not. Let me get you a towel and washcloth."

The hot water streaming over Fitz's body felt luxurious. *I could get used to this.* He stayed in just a little longer than he thought was proper. Stepping out, he realized he hadn't thought to get clean clothes. *Oh well, these can't be that dirty.*

Walking back into the den, he found Ben sitting at the computer, head slumped. He rubbed Ben's shoulder. "I think we need to sleep for a couple of hours. We're too old just to keep going."

Ben looked up, and Fitz could see the gears turning as he tried to wake up and process what was going on. "I think you're right," he managed. "You take the bed where Buffett is. I'll set an alarm for two hours from now."

Fitz found a blanket and looked at his watch: 4:41. He lay down without unmaking the bed, pulled the blanket over, and Buffett settled onto his chest. The next thing he knew, Ben was calling from the doorway. "Get up. I've found something." It was 7:53am.

Buffett scolded as Fitz threw off the blanket and hurried to the desk where Ben sat at the computer. He could tell it was an image of the Charger before getting close enough to see the screen well. "That's them!" A flash of excitement ran through him.

"This shows them at Jesse Jewell and Enota at three twenty-four this morning. I followed them up Three sixty-five to Highway Fifty-two. Then they came back down Three sixty-five and exited at One twenty-nine. I saw us following behind and the police car, too." Ben fast-forwarded the images so Fitz could see.

"Then what?" Fitz asked, praying for more.

"I lost them after they turned east on One twenty-nine. No more traffic cameras."

Disappointment dashed the hope that was building. Fitz dropped onto the couch, legs not wanting to hold him up anymore. Gears churned in his head, but the only thoughts that formed were, *I failed again. I failed again. I failed again.*

The last two days had been too much. *I have to get out of here.* He didn't realize he was pacing madly around the room.

"Are you OK?" Ben asked.

"I have to get out of here." He marched back to the bedroom and gathered Buffett and his supplies then headed to his car.

"What are you doing? We have to find Katía and Zee."

"I need some space," Fitz managed as he walked out the door with the first load. When he came back for the cat, Ben was back at the computer.

"I guess I'll have to do this without you. I can't believe you'd walk out on them," Ben huffed.

"I'm sorry."

Buffett sat in the passenger seat and glared at Fitz.

"I'm sorry. I just couldn't stay there anymore. I know it was comfortable. Quit giving me that look." He cranked the car and drove off.

* * * * *

Katía jumped up, startling Zee awake. Blue lights flashed through the front windows. "The police are here!"

"Sorry. I must have fallen asleep," Zee said. "Oh, I see. Blue lights."

"Someone must have heard my calls. Thank you, Lord."

A loud knock was followed by, "Hall County Sheriff. Open up."

"We're chained and can't get to the door. Come around to the back. I think it's unlocked," Katía shouted, hope surging in her heart. "We're saved, Zee."

"I'll believe it when I see it."

Katía heard the back door open. "Hall County Sheriff. I'm entering the house."

"We're in the hallway," Katía called. She could see a flashlight bobbing as the deputy entered the house.

"I got a call about someone disturbing the peace. They said it was coming from this location. Come out with your hands up."

"Disturbing the peace. So much for a compassionate soul hearing my calls."

"At least someone heard," Zee said. "We're in here officer. They have us chained and we can't come any farther."

"Get face-down on the floor," the deputy called.

"Good grief," Zee muttered.

"He's just being careful," Katía said. "OK, we're on the floor."

The light moved into the hallway. "Stay down and don't move." The deputy knelt and frisked Zee then Katía. He stepped back. "OK. You can get up."

"Thank God you came," Katía said. "We've been abducted by a gang called Confederate Rising. Can you get us free of these shackles?"

"You're the one who called from the park the other day. It's odd you should end up in this predicament," he said. "You really shouldn't be disturbing the neighbors like that."

"At least it got you here," she said. "They've run the chains through two-by-fours screwed into the walls. I think you'll need some tools."

"I'll be right back." The deputy went out the back door.

"I think that's Ron Carson. He's the deputy that came when the gang first tried to kidnap me."

"They tried to get you more than once?"

"Yeah. You know about the second time. The first time, I was taking pictures at the park when they came up. Fitz and Ben noticed what was going on and hurried over. The guy pulled a knife and threatened Fitz. Fitz pulled his gun and…" Katía froze and went silent. The blue lights turned off, and the deputy's car drove away.

"He just left us here," Zee said.

CHAPTER 36

Angry and frustrated, Ben walked back toward the computer. Snickers barked and King joined him.

"OK. It is morning isn't it?" He detoured to the back door and let them out. Then he prepared the dogs' food. *I think I need breakfast, too.* After letting the dogs back in, he poured himself a bowl of cereal and a fresh cup of coffee then settled back at the computer. *I can't believe Fitz just walked out.*

Feeling grumpy and stressed, he tried to figure out what else he could do. *I know when they took off and which way they headed back into town after they found the tracker. I'll try McEver Road and Dawsonville Highway at around that time. I sure hope I don't get in trouble for this.*

He located the footage from that traffic camera and began to watch. He was able to follow them down John Morrow Parkway across Jesse Jewell. His excitement built with each sighting.

"They turned left onto MLK!" He couldn't locate any more cameras till he got to Highway 129. He watched and watched, struggling to keep his eyes open. *No sign of them. They could have gone anywhere in there.*

Ben pulled up a map and studied the area. *There are endless possibilities. I guess the only thing to do is go have a look around.* He poured coffee into a thermos, donned his coat, and opened the garage door. At the last minute, he called the dogs. "Want to go for a ride?" Snickers and King barreled out the door.

He was nearly cross-eyed as he drove toward MLK, Jr. Blvd., and the coffee was still too hot to drink. The dogs kept their noses to the windows, swapping sides every minute or so.

He turned left onto MLK, intentionally following the gang's path. *Maybe I'll notice something. Maybe I'll see the car.* Driving all the way to Highway 129, he saw nothing. *I don't think there's anything past here that would interest them. Why would they come this way? To go out 129 without being seen on traffic cameras? No, there's one at this light, and I didn't see them pass. Maybe I should have looked longer.*

Waiting for the light to change, Ben dozed off, head landing on the headrest. He jumped at the sound of a horn behind him. The light was green, so he proceeded straight, crossing Highway 129. *I wonder how long I sat there. I need more sleep if I'm going to function.*

He aimed the car toward home and struggled through the fifteen minute drive. *I'll just have a short nap then get back at it.* He landed on the bed followed by the two dogs and was asleep before they could get settled.

* * * * *

Fitz didn't know where he was going when he left Ben's house. He knew he needed something but couldn't give voice to it. *I need space so I can think. I have to calm the anxiety. It's trying to take over. It has taken over. I don't owe Zee or Katia anything. Why should I stress out over them? I don't owe anyone anything except Buffett. I have to take care of him.*

"We're a team aren't we, Bud?" Buffett didn't respond. "Are you still judging me? I had to leave before I lost my mind." He looked, and Buffett had his back to him, facing the passenger door.

"Come on, Buffett. Give me a break." Guilt swirled with anxiety, fueling the stress he was feeling. "Don't make me stop and buy whiskey," he scolded the cat. Buffett remained statuesque.

That's the easy way out. I could just drink reality away. There's a convenience store. No whiskey, but they would have wine. He pulled into the parking lot and sat in front of the store waging war in his soul.

I can't do this. Don't throw five years of sobriety down the drain. But I need a drink. It will help me get past this. Then I can go back to sobriety. Just this once…

Buffett's paw rubbed across his cheek. He looked down to find the cat standing, one paw resting on his shoulder. Buffett rubbed his chin on Fitz's chin and purred.

A warm surge of love flowed through Fitz. He remembered the first time Buffett had done that. He was sitting behind Popeye's Chicken next to the dumpster, whiskey bottle in one hand and a drumstick he had found in the other. He had nearly passed out from the whiskey when a paw touched his face and roused him.

Opening his eyes, he saw a fluffy orange tabby cat looking up at him with huge eyes. The strange cat touched him again. Fitz had been touched by the compassion in those eyes and the tenderness of the paw. The interaction with the cat had brought him to enough to be able eat the piece of chicken, part of which he shared with the cat, and to throw the whiskey into the dumpster.

The cat followed him back to his tent. Fitz named him Buffett, and they'd been together ever since.

"You saved me from drinking once. It looks like you're going to do it again. Thanks." He pulled Buffett onto his lap and scratched his ears, eliciting serious purring. "OK. No booze. Now what?"

The convenience store was just down the road from Laurel Park. "Getting back into our routine might help." He drove through the park and went through the ritual of washing up, even though he'd showered earlier, replenishing Buffett's water, and scooping the litter. The familiar actions served to straighten the kinks out of his soul.

He heard footsteps and looked up to find Luna running over from the trail. "Any word on Zee?" she asked.

"Nothing but bad news." Fitz considered not telling her about Katía. *She'll find out anyway. Then she'll be mad that I didn't tell her.* "We lost Katía, too."

Her puzzled look told Fitz he would have to provide more details. "She got the idea that we could use her to find Zee. She posed as a homeless person, and they abducted her. She was wearing a tracking device, but they found it. They got away before we could get to her. Now we don't know where she is."

A rapid-fire stream of Spanish filled the air. Luna was pacing back and forth, hands on her hips. "Luna, you're speaking in Spanish. That doesn't help matters."

She threw her hands in the air. "I leave for a few days and look what happens. Two grown men don't have enough sense to stop Katía from placing herself in danger. What were you thinking?" She resumed her tirade in Spanish. Fitz could only imagine what she was saying.

Suddenly she stopped. "Now what do we do? Please tell me you called the police." Her hands landed on her hips again, and she faced Fitz with a fiery stare.

"Ben did call the police. There's another problem. I think someone in the sheriff's office is in on whatever is going on. It seems to be the deputy who has responded to our calls. He hasn't issued a BOLO or filed any reports about the abductions. Someone higher up could be involved, too."

"Well tell someone else!"

"I've tried to get the BOLO issued, but it has to come from an officer."

"Have you tried every single deputy in the sheriff's department? Have you talked to the sheriff?"

"No."

"Do you want to ride with me or drive? We're going to the sheriff's office."

"I don't think that's a good idea."

The fire was back in her glare. "Do you care to explain?"

"I don't know how high up the cover-up goes. We might just get the case buried deeper."

"So you're not even going to try? It can't get any worse."

"Actually it can. If we stir up a hornets' nest, we might get stung."

"What does that mean?"

"We could get locked away or worse. We need to find her on our own. As long as the powers that be think we've left it in their hands, they'll leave us alone."

"Do you really think our own sheriff's department is that corrupt?"

"I have no way of knowing. I'm ninety percent sure there's one involved, and if there's one involved, there are likely others."

"Where's Ben?" Hands landed back on her hips as she looked around.

I guess the truth is the best policy. "We were at his house. He hacked into the traffic camera footage and was trying to locate the gang members' car. I had an anxiety attack and had to leave." Fitz fully expected Luna to explode and go on another tirade. Instead, the fire in her eyes softened.

"Have you calmed down enough to get back to searching for her?"

Buffett meowed loudly enough to be heard through the car windows. "Buffett says I have."

"Let's go then. I'll follow you to Ben's."

Fitz's spine locked when Luna hopped into his passenger seat, scooting Buffett into her lap. The zing of anxiety passed, though, and he managed to drive her to her car.

CHAPTER 37

On the drive back to Ben's, Fitz plowed his mind for two things: ideas to help find Katía and Zee and remembering how to get to Ben's house. He passed the house before he realized it and had to turn around. Luna was following right behind.

He parked on the road in front of Ben's house, petted Buffett, and got out. Luna joined him, and they walked to the front door. Fitz knocked and waited. No answer, so he knocked again.

Luna reached around him and pushed the doorbell. "That's what these buttons are for."

The garage door started opening as Ben pulled in. Fitz and Luna met him in the garage.

"Hey," Fitz said, his voice thick with guilt.

"You brought reinforcements," Ben replied. "Hey, Luna."

"You look beat," she said.

"Thanks. I am beat. I thought I'd found something, but it didn't pan out."

"What did you think you had found?" Fitz asked.

"I tracked the car down MLK Boulevard. I drove down it but didn't find anything." Once the garage door was closed he let Snickers and King out. "I thought I'd come home and sleep a while. I wasn't expecting company."

The barb dug into Fitz's heart. "I'm sorry I left. Sometimes the anxiety is just too much. Buffett calmed me down. He has saved me more than once."

"I'm glad you're back."

"Me, too. How about showing me the footage you found, then you get some sleep and Luna and I will work for a while."

"Sounds good. I found this by following the route I assumed they took after they left the house with Katía." Ben showed them the shots of the car turning onto Martin Luther King, Jr. Boulevard.

"Did you see anything after that?" Luna asked.

"No. I watched the other end at Highway 129 for a few minutes but didn't see them come through there. Then I got excited and went to see if I could find the car."

"We know they were in Lula after that," Fitz said, observing the time stamp. What if they put her somewhere in that area of midtown? She might still be there even if they're not. Did you notice any abandoned houses?"

"I didn't see any, but I just went down MLK. It could be anywhere in that section of town."

"Let's pull up the map of houses we were looking at earlier. Are any targets in that area?"

Ben pulled up the map. "It looks like there are two possibilities, but it's a crowded area. I'm not sure they would use either of them."

Fitz was scribbling down the addresses. "You get some sleep, and we'll check these out." He headed toward the door then turned around. "Can we take the dogs?"

"Sure," Ben answered around a yawn.

"Let's get moving," Luna said.

They loaded the dogs, then Fitz took a deep breath and popped three M&Ms into his mouth before getting into Luna's car.

They checked out the two empty houses, finding nothing. The dogs didn't signal any unusual interest, either. "What do we do now?" Luna asked.

"Where else could they go around here? Let's drive down MLK and see if there are any empty buildings."

They loaded the dogs back into Luna's car. "Go to First Baptist Church by one twenty-nine and turn around so we can search the whole stretch," Fitz directed.

Luna drove slowly as Fitz's head rotated side to side. They passed businesses, homes, and apartments. Just before they got to Queen City Parkway, he said, "Turn around and let's look again."

Luna turned around and drove back the other way. "Stop! Back up!" Fitz shouted. "What's this?" There was a building that looked like it could have been some kind of shop on their right.

"What about it?" Luna asked, checking her mirror for oncoming traffic.

"There are no cars here. Pull in."

Luna turned into the parking area.

"Wait here while I check it out," Fitz said, opening the door.

"Yeah, right," Luna said, joining him.

"OK. If anyone's here, let's say we're looking for a furniture repair shop," Fitz said. He tried the door. "Locked. There aren't any windows. Let's look around the back." There were no windows in the back, either. "I have a funny feeling about this place. Let's get the dogs out."

Luna took King's leash, and Fitz took Snickers's. They led the dogs to the front door. King started barking and pulling on his leash. Snickers sniffed with enthusiasm.

"I think they're here," Luna said.

"At least Zee is… or was. I can't imagine any other reason for the dogs' behavior." Fitz took the door lever and pulled hard. It didn't budge. He banged on the door with the side of his fist. No response. He banged even harder.

"What if they're bound and gagged?"

"That's possible. We need to get in there. There's a handle lock and a deadbolt. It will take at least a crowbar. I might even have to cut away some of the metal."

"Can't you just pick the lock?"

Fitz nodded his head. "The tools are in my car, though, and that will take too long. Where's the nearest hardware store? Walmart? Let's go."

"How about that Harbor Freight store?" Luna asked as she loaded King into the back seat.

"Yeah! That's even closer."

Fitz located a crowbar, then found the battery powered cut-off tools. The sticker shock was powerful. "I think I'll see if the crowbar works first."

"I agree. If not, we'll come back, and I'll buy this thing."

When they got back to the building, it was no longer empty. A car was in the parking lot.

"It looks like we won't need this after all." Fitz slid the crowbar onto the back seat floorboard. "Remember, we're looking for a furniture repair shop."

Fitz tugged on the door, but it was still locked. He shot a puzzled look at Luna, then knocked. The twisting of the deadbolt preceded the door cracking open.

"Can I help you?" asked a White male with a shaved head.

"I hope so. We've been looking all over for this furniture repair shop. I'm hoping we've found it." He smiled trying to sell his ruse.

"Nope. Can't help you." The door shut, and the lock twisted.

CHAPTER 38

Fitz stared at the door then looked to Luna. His mental gears were turning so fast they left him with a blank expression.

"That was odd. I'd say he's hiding something. We need to get inside! They could be here," Luna said. She stepped toward the door, but Fitz blocked her way.

"It's too risky. If they have them, they'll figure out we're onto them."

"We have to do something! We can't just walk away and leave them! We might be so close!"

Fitz had his finger to his lips, trying to quiet Luna. "Let's get back into the car," he calmly requested, then led Snickers to the back seat.

Fitz was worried when Luna stood defiantly in place. Finally she said, "Come on, King," and stomped to the car. Fitz felt relieved. *I hope they don't have audio feeds. On video, we probably just look like a couple fighting over furniture.*

"What do we do now?" she asked. "We should call the police."

"I don't know how far up this cover-up goes. We can't trust the police."

"We have to do something. Do you have a gun? We could force them to let us in," Luna suggested.

Fitz rubbed his forehead. "I do have a gun. Whoever is in there probably does, too. And we don't know how many of them there are. I think what we need to do is stake out this place."

"You mean just sit here and watch it? Don't you think they'll notice we're in the parking lot?" Luna rubbed her hands down her thighs.

"I mean park somewhere inconspicuous and watch. They have security cameras, so we'd need a different vehicle."

Luna cranked the car and drove out of the lot. "Should we use yours or Ben's?"

"I think I'll come back in mine. Let's let Ben rest. I'll let both of you know if anything happens." *I hope she takes the hint. I'm not sure I could bear the strain of being penned up with someone right now.* He surveyed the street for an inconspicuous place to park.

Back at Ben's, Fitz sat down in his car and Buffett jumped into his lap. Tension flowed out of his body. "It feels good to be home," he said to the cat.

"Meow." Buffett rubbed chins with him.

"Are you up for a mission? We have to do a stake out."

Buffett lay down on his lap and purred. "As long as it comes with a nap in my lap you're good. I see." Fitz drove back to MLK and parked in a sunny spot about a tenth of a mile from the shop. Buffett was still in his lap.

Fitz shifted his weight to get more comfortable and leaned his head back against the headrest. Buffett stood, stretched, did a complete turn, and lay back down. The car was still parked at the building, right where it had been.

Fitz dug out a granola bar and his water bottle. Munching on the granola bar, he kept his eyes on the front door. Watching an unadorned building with nothing happening was dull. The sun warmed the car. With Buffett in his lap he was comfortable… content, even. The stress of having friends in harm's way and all of the close company had worn on his soul. He scratched the cat's neck.

Fitz awoke gradually, as if consciousness had to ooze through molasses. Eyes scanning the scene in front of the car, he slowly remembered where he was and what he had been doing. He stiffened when he realized the car was gone. "I missed them!" The loudness of his voice prompted Buffett to jump to the other seat.

Panic oozed into Fitz's nerves, slowly building. It was arrested by a new thought, *This might be an opportunity instead of a crisis.* He started digging through his memory while he rummaged through the glove box for the pouch of lock picking tools, trying to recall the steps he had learned in law enforcement training.

I think I can remember the strategies. It wasn't until he got out of the car that he noticed a note taped to the windshield. "WE'RE WATCHING YOU!," it read. "Well good, because I'm watching you, too."

He started toward the building then thought about the surveillance cameras. *If someone's monitoring the cameras, I could be arrested before I get inside. But if I'm fast enough, I could get in and out before the police arrive. Of course, there could still be someone in there.* He paused to puzzle through the conundrum. *It's worth the risk.*

After taking off the safety on his Beretta, he hurried to the building. Not even bothering to check, he started with the deadbolt. *This will be the hardest.*

The lock yielded to his machinations, and he slid a thin piece of metal in to release the latch. He hesitated before opening the door, listening. *I have to hurry.*

Yanking the door open, he hurried in, Beretta at the ready. He didn't bother closing the door and moved through the dark building, wishing his eyes would hurry up and adjust to the lower light. He bumped into a counter that seemed to be where a receptionist might have sat, moved to the right, and found a closed door.

He put his ear to the door. Hearing no sound, he jerked it open and rushed in, looking left and right as he moved down a hallway. When he reached the end of the hallway, he was confused by what he had seen. Relaxing a bit at the realization that no one was there, he went back, looking more closely. *Is this a medical facility? It looks like a small hospital.*

He noticed four bedrooms and what looked like an operating room. *I think I made a big mistake.* He turned on the flashlight app and made one more trip down the hallway. A shiny reflection caught his attention in one of the rooms. He went in and found a chain attached to the bed with a handcuff on the other end.

No, this was no mistake. He erased his earlier fear that he might have invaded a legitimate business. *What are they doing here? It can't be good. I have to find Zee and Katia before it's too late. But right now I have to get out.*

He hustled out of the building, shut the door, and headed for his car. It wasn't till the frigid air seeped through his coat that he realized how much he had been sweating.

* * * * *

"Hey, Boss. We have a problem," Gene said, nervously drumming his fingers on the counter. He dreaded sharing the news about the break-in but knew it would be worse not to.

"What is it," the impatient voice asked.

"A man broke into the lab."

"What! How? Why did that happen?" the response exploded over the phone.

"It's an old man. He came earlier saying he was looking for a furniture store. He broke in later, after Jack had left." Gene stopped drumming his fingers, bracing for the tongue lashing.

The silent pause dragged on. Finally, "Find him and eliminate him."

CHAPTER 39

Fitz turned his car around and drove away from the building so the cameras couldn't pick up his tag number. He was trying to process what he had seen and figure out where to go. It was then that a sobering thought struck. *If this is some kind of illegal operation, they won't call the police… They'll come after me themselves.* He had to force his foot not to press down too hard on the accelerator.

"Buffett, what should we do next?"

"Meow."

"Great idea. I need to pull over somewhere and ponder this. And there just happens to be an Arby's up ahead."

Buffett perked up and meowed again upon hearing the word, Arby's. Fitz rubbed down the cat's back. "You do like a Beef N Cheddar, don't you."

"Meow."

Fitz's stomach rumbled as he placed his order at the drive-thru contraption. After paying and collecting the bag, he pulled into a parking space. The first thing he did was to tear some of the roast beef off and place it on the sack for Buffett.

"Servants always eat after their masters," he chuckled. As his hunger subsided, the pressure of finding Zee and Katía escalated. "What are they going to do to them? I have to find them before something terrible happens. What if it has already happened? I think it's time for Ben to wake up." Despite Fitz's questions, Buffett's only response was licking his lips.

He finished the sandwich, then drove to Ben's house. He rang the doorbell, then banged on the door.

"I'm not deaf, you know," Ben said, opening the door.

"I thought you might still be asleep."

They walked into the kitchen where Ben had his computer set up on the counter, an empty plate beside it. "Want some iced tea?" he asked.

"That would be great. Thanks." Fitz noticed the *Gainesville Times* on the counter. The headline read, "BODY FOUND IN WOODS." Picking up the paper he said, "What's this?"

"I don't know. Haven't read it yet."

Fitz began scanning the article. His breath caught when he read that the body appeared to have recently had brain surgery.

"You look spooked. What does it say?" Ben asked.

"They found a Black male in the woods near the site where they're developing that new inland port."

"And?" Ben encouraged.

"It says he had brain surgery not too long before he died. They haven't been able to identify the body."

"That's sad."

"It's terrifying! While you were asleep, Luna and I found a building on MLK, and the dogs acted like they could smell Zee. We tried to get in, but the guy closed the door on us. I went back to stake out the place. After they left, I broke in, and it looked like a small hospital, complete with an operating table."

"You broke into a building?" Ben asked, pausing with the glass of tea halfway to his mouth.

"I needed to see if Zee and Katía were in there."

"You know that's illegal, right?"

"I know the law," Fitz grumped. "Don't you see? This man's fate could be the same as what Zee and Katía are headed for." Fitz's heart was racing.

Ben seemed frozen. He looked at Fitz with a blank expression. Finally he said, "We have to find them before it's too late."

"There's one more caveat. They saw me at the stake out and had video surveillance in operation when I broke in. They will probably be after me." *I don't see any point in mentioning that I fell asleep at the stake out.*

"You probably should have thought about that before you broke in. Now what can we do? I've been going through the street camera footage but haven't seen anything since last night." He took a sip of tea.

"I'm sure our goons are all tucked up in their beds. They're creatures of the night."

"What would you do if you were on the force investigating this?"

"I would have issued a BOLO a long time ago, and the creeps would have been apprehended by now," Fitz snapped.

Ben put his glass onto the counter. "I didn't mean to offend you. What would you do now, given the gang is still at large?"

"Sorry. I'm not snapping at you. I'm just frustrated. It's hard when law enforcement is working against you."

"Is there anyone on the force you still trust? Who might be willing to help?"

Fitz searched his mind but could not identify anyone except Geraldine. "Geraldine is the only one I know, but she is a secretary. I need to think." Fitz crossed to the den area, which was open to the kitchen, and sat in a recliner. Leaning back he closed his eyes to seek a plan in his mind.

Ben returned to the computer. Within three minutes, he heard snoring. *It looks like the guy needs some sleep.*

Fitz awoke disoriented. A surge of fear washed through as he scanned the surroundings. It wasn't until he saw Ben hunched over the computer that he remembered where he was. As his mind cleared, the memory of a dream surfaced.

He was standing on a rope bridge that was swinging in the wind and looking down to a river. He could see Katía in some sand on the side. She was sinking. Two of the gang members were standing nearby, one holding a rope. He would throw it just short of where Katía could reach it and laugh as he pulled it back. Fitz started running to get to Katía, but the bridge was so long he could never get to the end of it.

Fitz stretched and stood up, the dream adding even more urgency to the need for a plan.

"You didn't sleep very long," Ben said.

"Bad dream. I need to stay awake long enough to come up with a plan."

"Maybe we can grab one of the goons as they come out of the bar and force him to tell us where they are," Ben offered.

"That might be a possibility." Fitz weighed the pitfalls of the plan. *One, there are four of them and two of us. I could get the jump on them by having my gun ready. Two, it would put Ben on their radar. His life would be in danger, too. Three, if a police officer happened by, we could end up in jail. Four, if the leader pulls his gun, at least one of us will die.*

Fitz eyed Ben, trying to size up whether he would be game for the risks. "It would be risky, including gunfire and the possibility of our being killed. Or we could end up in jail if an officer happens by. Thirdly, you will have a target on your back just like me."

"I've lived through my wife dying of cancer. I think I can handle it. Besides, if I die, I'll get to be with her again."

"Right now, that's the best option I see for rescuing Zee and Katía. I'm giving that gun back to you."

CHAPTER 40

The time was 12:53pm. "It's a long time till four o'clock," Ben noted. "Why don't I see if I can follow that car you saw at the shop?"

"Good idea," Fitz agreed.

"Did you see which way they went?"

"No."

Ben eyed him with a puzzled look. Fitz's gut squirmed. "OK. I fell asleep. I'll admit it."

"I'm glad to know you're human like the rest of us. I'll start at Highway 129. Do you remember what time you started your stake out?"

"I think it was around ten-fifteenish." Fitz spied his empty tea glass, but the coffee maker called instead. He retrieved the mug he'd used earlier from the sink. Ben sank his attention into the computer.

"What kind of car was it?"

"A gray Nissan Altima," Fitz replied as he placed the mug into the microwave.

"Did you get the tag number?"

A flash of failure wormed into Fitz's heart. "No. I guess I was so surprised by the door getting shut in my face that I didn't think to do that."

"Got one! It's turning right onto 129. I won't be able to follow it from there."

Another surge of failure hammered Fitz's heart. "The rule of thumb is we only have twenty-four hours to find the victim after an abduction. It's been ten days since Zee went missing and our twenty-four hours are about up on Katía."

"You know, I bet her family doesn't even know what happened. We need to get in touch with them." Ben rested his head in his hands.

"How are we going to do that? I don't know her family. I don't even remember the name of the church she pastors."

Ben looked up wide-eyed. "I don't either. We need to get to know each other better."

"When this is over you can throw us a get better acquainted party, but for now we need to focus on getting her and Zee back."

Fitz was flustered. He looked around the room as if a plan might be lying on an end table. *Ben keeps a neat house.* The news was on the TV, playing low in the background. "The news! The newspaper! Let's go!"

"What are you talking about?"

"Let's see if we can get the newspaper to run a story on this."

"It will take days for them to get it into the paper. That'll be too late."

"But they could get it online today if they wanted to."

Ben jumped up from the counter. "You're right! Let's go!" He was halfway out the door before Fitz realized he was leaving. He hurried to catch up.

It was 1:30pm on the dot when they arrived at the Gainesville Times building. Walking toward the front door, Fitz said, "Maybe you should do the talking. You look more respectable."

Ben looked Fitz over.

"Don't say I should wait in the car," Fitz grumped.

"I would never suggest such a thing."

They walked into the building, and a smart looking woman with straightened black hair and wearing a khaki business suit was crossing the lobby. "Fitz? Is that you?"

"Hey, Serena."

"What brings you to the Times? I always had to track you down for an interview."

"We have an urgent story that needs to get out. Serena, this is Ben, a friend of mine."

"I'm glad to know you've made a friend," she chuckled. "Come on back and let's talk about this story. I interviewed Fitz for stories on some of the crimes committed in our area. He wasn't the most forthcoming of souls," she explained to Ben.

"I can believe that," Ben replied.

Serena rolled a third chair up to her desk, sat down, and asked, "What's going on?"

"We have two friends who have been abducted. One, Zaderian Jameson, is a homeless guy who disappeared about ten days ago," Fitz looked to Ben for confirmation. Ben nodded his head.

"The other is a pastor at one of the Gainesville churches. Her name is Katía…"

"Bancroft," Ben interjected.

"Thanks. She was abducted yesterday evening. We haven't been able to locate either of them." He decided to leave out the part about the tracking device for now. "We also found some kind of medical facility in an old shop on Martin Luther King, Junior Boulevard that I'm sure is connected with the kidnappings."

Serena was writing furiously. When the pen stopped she looked up. "What have the police said about these abductions?"

"There's another problem. There seems to be a cover-up going on. A source at the sheriff's office told me that there haven't been any reports filed on these abductions."

Serena turned an incredulous gaze on Fitz. He could tell she was trying to process how to respond. She put her pen down and looked to Ben.

"He's telling the truth," Ben confirmed.

"These are serious accusations, Fitz. Are you sure you're not just trying to get revenge on the sheriff's department?"

"Serena, you know I've always shot straight with you. This is no different. We need to get this story out there to get the public's help with finding these people before it's too late," Fitz pleaded.

"It would also help alert others to be on guard against these goons," Ben added.

"You know I can't just willy nilly run a story. I'll have to do some research first."

"I understand. But could you at least put out a plea to help locate Zee and Katía? We have the make, model, and tag number of the abductors' car."

"One more thing. Do you remember the story of the dead African American male found at the inland port site? That was probably some of this gang's work," Ben added.

Serena's eyes narrowed as she studied Fitz. Finally she said, "OK. I'll run it by the editor and see what he says. After that, I'm going to dig into your allegations regarding the sheriff's department."

"Don't forget about the medical facility on MLK," Ben added.

CHAPTER 41

Max Herringer scoured the notes he'd made from his latest research, rubbing his temples as he thought. *I have to succeed this time. Max Herringer doesn't fail. I want to get this published by early summer.*

The intercom buzzed. "It's Dr. Cole, sir," Janice, Herringer's secretary said.

"Thanks. Take a message and tell him I'll call back." He knew Janice would create an excuse for him. *Cole's going to drive me nuts with his pestering. I shouldn't have told him I'd include him.*

He went back to his notes, checking to see if he had missed anything that might risk the next procedure's success. Impatience outmaneuvered caution, and he picked up the phone.

"I'm ready for the next procedure. Nine o'clock tomorrow morning. I trust you have a subject ready… A woman, you say. Well, that won't matter. Bring her in and get her ready."

* * * * *

Dawn broke on a hopeless morning. Katía had slept off and on briefly during the long night. Her ankle was sore from the handcuff. She stayed still, hoping Zee could get some sleep. She and Zee were arm to arm, leaning against the wall in the hallway. Zee had draped his coat over both of them. She was still cold.

Her mind was busier than her body. *Will they just leave us here to rot? There has to be a reason why they abducted us. How can we get out of here?*

Zee snorted and stretched. "I ache down to my bones, and I'm cold. How are you?"

"The same. I wish I knew what they were planning to do with us."

"It seems like they mentioned something about a doctor, but that might just be my imagination. My memory's not so good, you know. I'm hungry. I wonder if they left any of those granola bars." He grunted and groaned till he managed to stand.

Katía felt for him. *He shouldn't have to go through this. He's too old. Neither of us should be going through this. I'd better get up and help him hunt.*

"Great. It's the same flavor as last time," Zee called from the kitchen. "I don't see any water, though."

Katía joined him. "Let's see if the water's on." Turning the tap, she was relieved to see water streaming out.

"I wonder why they leave the water on in these dumps," Zee mused.

They tore into the granola bars, then drank from the faucet. The sun seemed to be weighed down, taking forever to climb up the sky. Sometime in late afternoon, Katía awoke to the sound of crunching gravel in the driveway.

The door opened, revealing Boomer holding blankets. Moe followed carrying two air mattresses. Boomer dropped the blankets just within Katía's reach.

"You have to let us go! This isn't right!" she yelled.

"Just be patient. You have an appointment with the good doctor in the morning," Ernie said with an evil grin. "Then maybe I'll get to play with you."

A wave of nausea hit Katía hard. Ernie's tone and expression were sickening. They were gone before she could ask what the doctor was going to do.

"What's that?" Zee asked, pointing to one of the packages.

"Air mattresses. It'll be a relief from these hard floors. Let's get them blown up." As she opened the packages, she realized there was no pump. "Great. No pump." When she grabbed the scroungy blankets, a hand pump fell out. She hooked it up and began pumping, thankful for something to do besides worrying.

As she pumped, she remembered reading about medical experiments on Black men in Alabama. "You don't think this is another Tuskegee thing, do you?"

Zee's blank expression told her he didn't know about the evil experiment. "It was when the government withheld treatment for syphilis from Black men to see how it would affect them. They kept it running from 1932 to 1972, all the while telling these men they were receiving free treatment for bad blood. White people let them suffer all that time."

"I hope it's not like that. But whatever it is, it can't be good."

* * * * *

Fitz and Ben left the newspaper building at 3:37pm. "We couldn't have timed that any better," Ben noted. They hopped into his car and drove the short distance to the bar.

"I'm getting good at this parallel parking," Ben said, nailing it on the first try.

"What if they don't show today?" Fitz asked more to himself than to Ben. He was trying to come up with a contingency plan.

Ben slapped his hand on the steering wheel, startling Fitz. "Why didn't I think of that before?"

"Think of what?"

"The Newtown Florist Club! They would certainly be willing to help get eyes searching for these guys. That rhymed, did you notice?"

"You're quite the poet, but how is a flower club going to help."

"Really? How can you not know about the Newtown Florist Club? It started after the thirty-six tornado as a group that provided flowers in the event of a death in that community. Now it's mostly a community action group that focuses on African American issues in this town."

Ben was tapping on his phone. "They close at four. I'm calling them." He clicked on the phone number listed on the search result.

Fitz could see Ben deflating. "It's their voicemail," he said.

"Go ahead and leave the information. Maybe someone will check it."

Ben explained the situation and left the tag number and description of the car. "If you could, please help us get the word out and let me know if anyone spots this car. I would be grateful. We are trying to save two of our friends." He disconnected the call.

"They picked a fine day to skip out early."

Ben just nodded. "I hope the goons stick to their routine. I'm ready for this ordeal to be over."

"Me, too. Will you be able to shoot one of them if it comes to that?" Fitz asked.

"I hope so," Ben answered, eyeing the Beretta Fitz had given him.

"Maybe it won't come to that, but it might. You need to decide ahead of time. In the moment is the wrong time to be trying to decide if you will kill a man."

CHAPTER 42

Ben straightened in his seat. "There they are." He reached for the door handle.

"Wait. They'll be easier to handle after they've had a couple of drinks."

"That's going to be a long wait."

Fitz nodded his head as he tried to picture in his mind how to handle the situation. He ran through three scenarios when he noticed Ben wiping his palms on his thighs. "Nervous?"

"Yep."

"Do you want to stay in the car?"

"Yep, but I can't let you try this on your own. You'll need help."

Fitz sank back into his thoughts, worrying that Ben might be a liability. Ben's eyes were glued to the mirror. He leaned forward, then relaxed. "False alarm," he said as a lone man walked out of the bar. "He must have forgotten something because he went back in."

"Get ready. They may have sent him out as a scout."

"Why would they do that?" Ben asked.

"To see if we are waiting for them."

The door to the bar burst open, and the four thugs raced to their car. "They're out!" Ben said.

Fitz jumped out of the car as fast as he could. Ben hesitated but followed on his heels. As they ran toward the Charger, it pulled away from the curb.

"Suckers!" one of the men called from the back seat. Then two shots rang out.

"My car!" Ben gasped and hurried back to find the two street-side tires flat.

"At least they didn't cause any body damage."

"I'm calling the police. They can't get away with that." He whipped out his phone.

"Let's think this through," Fitz cautioned. "You would have to explain why they shot out your tires."

"That's exactly what I'll do, except I'll leave out the part about our planning to abduct one of them."

"If the responding officer is part of the cover up, we could end up in jail for some made up cause. I think we need to call a tire company instead of the police."

Ben kicked one of the tires and started walking down the street.

"Where are you going?"

"Come on. I use Harrison Tire, and they're right down here. What if they say it's too late for them to do this? I was going to get new tires on the next rotation anyway."

Fitz hurried along, listening to Ben talk. He was paying more attention to trying to figure out their next move.

The man behind the counter griped and complained about how late it was but finally said they would replace Ben's tires.

Ben handed over the keys, and the man called to have a truck meet them at the car.

Fitz was staring out the window, lost in his thoughts when, "You coming?" filtered through. He followed Ben back to the car with his mind galloping. *What are we going to do? I have to take panic out of the picture and think clearly. We have to find… I'm panicking again. Think rationally, Fitz. What would the jerks be planning to do tonight?*

A truck from Harrison Tire parked on the road just past Ben's car. "How in tarnation did you get two flats at the same time? I'm Jim. Nice to meet you." the tire guy said as he cranked the generator.

"Some jerks drove by and shot them," Ben said.

Jacking up the car, Jim said, "Holes in the sidewalls. Those'll have to be replaced."

"That's the plan. I need all four replaced, but I can come back tomorrow for the other two."

"That's kind of ya."

Fitz wasn't paying attention. *OK, they have been abducting someone every few days. If I assume it's for some kind of medical thing, then there is probably a doctor involved who is running the show. Or it could be some kind of pharmaceutical company. But brain surgery? Why would they do brain surgery and then kill the man? They couldn't have a survivor who could tell what had happened. They're going to kill Zee and Katia.* Panic returned as he followed Ben back to the tire company.

Sitting in the waiting room, Fitz knew he should tell Ben what he had concluded but didn't want to worry him any more than he already was. He resumed pondering. *Why would they stop by that building but not leave Katia and Zee? We spooked them out of their last house, and they stored them there while they hunted down another? That makes sense. Could these guys just be hunters? Could they just abduct the people and then deliver them to the facility? If that's the case, they will probably be out hunting tonight. But where?*

What are they doing in that building? I need to find out but how?

Fitz noticed Ben studying his phone. Curiosity drew him from his thoughts, and he asked, "What are you working on so hard there?"

"I'm looking at empty houses where they might be holding them."

"Do you see anything?"

"Nothing different from what we found the other night. That seems so long ago, but it was just last night."

"I think we need to see what's going on in that facility. The question is how?"

"That's easy," Ben said.

Fitz eyed him like he'd lost his mind. "How is it easy?"

"We just break in and plant a camera of our own."

"You think that sounds easy?" Fitz was flummoxed. "They'd be watching our every move on their cameras."

"Not if we disable them."

Fitz scrunched his eyes, trying to figure out how to do that. "OK, I give. How would you disable them?"

"They most likely have only one exterior camera aimed at the parking lot. All we would have to do is come from the back of the building, stay close to the side, climb up, and cut the wire."

"OK, that sounds reasonable. But I saw cameras inside, too. Could we take them out?"

"Not directly, but the exterior camera is hooked up to a computer. We could send a jolt of electricity through the line and fry the computer. Whoever is monitoring the images would see only black. Of course, if it's a cellular system, we're screwed. I don't suppose you noticed what kind of camera they're using."

"I wouldn't have been able to tell even if I had looked."

"Did you see a wire coming from it?"

"I was too busy trying to get in. I didn't pay attention." Fitz noticed his voice was getting louder. The two men behind the counter glanced in his direction. "I'm sorry. I guess I feel defensive about not noticing those details."

"No problem. We'll have to have a look to find out."

CHAPTER 43

Armed with a step ladder and a tiny cellular camera just purchased from Best Buy, Fitz directed Ben to park a block behind the building that housed the medical facility. It was 7:43pm and dark.

"People will think it odd that we're walking down the street with a step ladder," Ben said as he finished his last bite of waffle fries from the Chik-Fil-A they had just visited.

"That's true. We don't want to linger once we get the ladder untied." Fitz ran his fingers through his beard checking for crumbs.

They pulled the ladder from the top of Ben's car. Fitz looked both ways, then led Ben across the lot of the building that backed up to the shop.

He paused at the corner, studying the shop. "Do you see any cameras?"

"Nope, but it's dark, so it's hard to tell."

Fitz drew his Beretta with his right hand, holding one end of the ladder with his left. "Let's go."

They stepped out from the corner of the building, having sufficient light from the surrounding buildings and street lights to make their way. Once they reached the side of the shop, Fitz stopped and searched the corners at the top of the building for cameras.

"It looks like we're in luck," he said.

"Remember to stay close to the building when we get to the front so the camera won't see you. We'll need to turn the ladder upright so it won't stick out. They may have a motion detection light, too."

"I know that," Fitz answered, insulted that the novice was lecturing him. He peeked around the corner. "No cars," he whispered.

They stood the ladder up and hugged the building as they rounded the corner. Placing the ladder under the camera, Fitz said, "You should be the one to go up since you know more about cameras than I do."

Ben started up the ladder and a security light at the peak of the roof came on. They both froze. "Motion detector," Ben whispered before resuming his climb. Reaching the top, he shook his head. It was a cellular camera.

"Take out the battery?" Fitz whispered up.

Ben had to feel to find the access to the battery compartment then popped it out. "One camera down. Now what?" he said as he descended the ladder.

"I guess we wave at them when we're inside."

"You realize they'll probably find the camera we place."

"Yeah, but it will be less likely if we give them something else to worry about."

"Like what?"

"I'll know it when I see it." Fitz moved to the front door. "Hold your light on the lock." He proceeded to unlock the door as he had before. It seemed harder in the dark.

As he struggled, the door popped open, knocking Fitz to the ground, and a man with a handgun stuck his head out.

"They said you'd be back." He aimed the gun at Fitz's chest.

Ben, being behind the open door, slammed into it with all his might crunching the man between the door and the frame. At least two ribs cracked, and he fell to the ground.

"Thanks," Fitz said, scrambling to snatch the man's gun. He noticed the Confederate flag tattooed on his neck. He pulled off the man's baseball cap and handed it to Ben. "Put that on. You get back inside."

They followed the man into the building and shut the door. Looking around for cameras, Fitz was surprised to see none. "Have a seat and don't move," he growled at the man. "What next?" he asked of Ben. Ben had already moved beyond the reception room.

"What are they doing in this place?" Fitz barked to his prisoner.

"They didn't tell me. I was just supposed to guard the building because they knew you'd be back."

"I don't believe you. How could you be a part of the gang and not know?"

"Gene don't tell anybody more than they need to know. He says it protects us."

"You don't look very protected," Fitz snapped. "I have a good mind to go ahead and put you out of my misery." He aimed the gun.

"Don't shoot!" the man yelped. "I'm telling you the truth."

Fitz was inclined to believe him. "OK, for now you're safe. Let's talk about my friends."

"What about your friends?"

Fitz liked the flash of fright he saw in the man's eyes. "Where are they holding Zee and Katía?"

"I have no idea what you're talking about."

Fitz lashed out and popped the guy on the back of the hand he was holding delicately over his ribs. Over the man's yelp, Fitz said, "Does that help you remember?"

The man cowered away from Fitz, eyes wide.

"I can do that again if it helps."

"I don't know no Zee or Katía."

"Your friends kidnapped them and are holding them somewhere. All you have to do is tell me where, and I'll go away and leave you alive."

The man tried to scoot farther away, but the arm of the chair blocked him. "I swear I don't know. Gene don't talk about things. He keeps it to himself. Says if one of us gets caught, the others are spared." He had both arms shielding his ribs.

Fitz glared at him and decided he was telling the truth. "Shut up… Is there anything I can help you with, Ben?"

"Making good progress. Just keep the goon at bay."

Fitz noticed a smirk on the man's face. "Goon face says we don't have much time. He must have called someone. Have you found the computer yet?"

"Oh, yeah. It's ours."

Bangs and crashes sounded from the back. "What are you doing?" Fitz called.

"Tidying up. I have everything we came for," Ben said, walking back into the reception room.

"You want us to call you an ambulance?" Fitz asked.

"No. I'm good," the man groaned.

"Let's put you to bed, then." Fitz directed him back toward the rooms with beds. He noticed equipment scattered on the floor. "Nice job of tidying."

"Thank you," Ben replied.

Fitz used the handcuff already attached and cuffed the man to the bed. "Sweet dreams."

He and Ben hurried out of the building and back to the car. "I hope he bought the idea that we were just after the computer," Ben said.

"Me, too." They tied the ladder on top of the Outback and drove off. Two minutes later a phone rang.

"That must be yours," Fitz said.

"Nope. It's the goon's. I borrowed it." Ben pulled it out of his pocket and handed it to Fitz.

Fitz puzzled a second then decided to answer. "Hello."

"What's going on over there? They said the cameras went off."

"Gene, is that you?"

"You know it's me! Now what's going on?"

"It's so kind of you to call and check on me. I'm not feeling so well."

"You don't sound like Freddy. Who is this?"

"I'm the thorn in your side, and I'm about to dig in deep." Fitz disconnected the call and turned off the phone.

CHAPTER 44

Ben pulled into the parking lot at First Baptist Church on MLK, Jr. Drive and pulled out his phone. "Let's see if the camera is working," he said, opening the app. "Perfect." He handed the phone to Fitz.

"Nice. We can see the operating table and out into the hallway. I'd say you've done this before."

Ben grinned. "The app will store the footage in the cloud so we can look over it whenever we want."

"I see it has audio, too."

"Yep."

"The sound of this guy groaning is music to my ears." Fitz said.

"Do you think we should park away from the building and see if the Charger shows up?"

"That's exactly what I was thinking. Are you up for another long night?"

"The spirit's willing but the flesh is weak. I hope the flesh can stay awake." Ben groaned.

"Let's park in the lot we just left. We can see the entrance from there."

As Ben drove back to the parking lot of the building behind the facility, Fitz wondered about him. *I think Ben knows more than he's letting on. He knew exactly what to do in that situation. He was positioned where he needed to be when the guy slung the door open, then took him out in one move. He doesn't seem to want to talk about it though. I'll ask later.*

Ben parked in the shadow of a tree that just barely allowed a view of the entrance to the other lot. "Maybe they won't notice us here," he said.

Fitz eyed him. *My previous thoughts have just been confirmed. I wish I had another Arby's sandwich.*

They waited in silence, each lost in thought until they saw lights pulling into the parking lot.

"That's them," Fitz said.

Ben still had the camera feed open, and he held the phone so they both could see. The lights came on in the hallway. Gene walked in and looked around. "Go check on Freddy. The boss isn't going to like this. Hey, Ernie, go check the computer and see if you can figure out who did this. We're going to return the favor."

He looked to the one guy still standing there. "Start cleaning this mess up and put everything where it belongs. Boomer, get back in here and help Moe clean up." Gene walked out of sight. All they could hear was the noise of the two men picking up what Ben had tossed onto the floor.

"Maybe I shouldn't have trashed the place. It's just slowing them down," Ben said.

"True, but it helps sell the idea that we were after their computer," Fitz replied.

Watching the guys clean up got tedious. They noticed Gene walk by with Freddy, expletives lighting up the audio. "I don't think Gene is happy about the situation," Fitz observed.

"Poor fellows," Ben quipped. "Should we go help them clean up?"

Fitz laughed. "No, I think they deserve this."

"The computer's gone. They stole it," they heard someone call.

"From Freddy's description, it sounds like the two guys that have been bugging us. When we see them again we'll shoot them instead of their tires," they heard Gene say.

"We'd better be careful," Ben said. "I think he was serious about shooting us."

"Yeah, he seems touchy like that." They laughed.

"Put it back neatly. You know the boss can't stand a mess. He wants it organized," Gene ordered, peering through the doorway.

"I don't know where this stuff goes," Boomer griped.

"Freddy, get in here and tell them where to put stuff," Gene called.

"But I'm hurting."

"Shut up and get in here."

"It looks like we're going to be here a while," Fitz said, leaning back in the seat. He tried to relax the stiffness out of his muscles.

"I can't wait till we find these guys. I want to do more than shoot them," Boomer griped. "They need to suffer slow and hard."

Ben shifted in his seat. "I think they really want to hurt us."

Fitz nodded his head.

"I wonder if we should get a different car," Ben said.

"The rental places are all closed now. Besides, we would risk losing them if we left."

"I was actually thinking of Luna's Forerunner."

Fitz leaned forward and stroked his beard. "That's a promising idea if she could drive it to us in time. But I hate putting her at risk."

"There's no risk if they don't see her," Ben pressed.

"There is if they see the tag," Fitz countered. *I can't believe he's willing to put Luna in jeopardy.*

"Careful!" Gene yelled. "This stuff is for a medical procedure. It has to stay sterile."

"Our suspicions are confirmed. But is the procedure brain surgery?" Fitz wondered.

"Hurry up, too. The boss is planning to do another one in the morning." It was Gene again. "It's the woman this time."

"That has to be Katía," Ben said.

"I agree. We have to find her before morning."

Fitz and Ben watched in silence as the men straightened up the bins Ben had tossed.

Finally, Ben said, "I don't think Luna has time to get here anyway." Fitz's anger at Ben eased.

"Let's go. We have a volunteer to deliver," Gene directed.

"What about me?" Freddy asked.

"You need to stay here. We don't have room for you."

"But I'm hurting."

Gene leered at Freddy. "Well find some pain medicine and take it, you idiot." With that, Gene led the other three out of the building.

Ben didn't make a move to crank the Outback until the others were in the Charger with the doors closed. "Don't worry, I have the lights off." They watched as the Charger headed north on MLK.

Ben pulled out of the parking lot and took the road parallel and one block east of MLK. He turned left onto Grove Street then made a right onto MLK. The Charger was about five hundred feet ahead of them.

"Don't lose them," Fitz said nervously. "This might be our only chance."

"I wonder what they're going to do to her if we can't stop them."

"I don't want to think about it." Fitz was sweating when they pulled behind the Charger at the red light at Athens Highway. He set the Beretta in his lap.

The light finally changed, and they followed the Charger across Highway 129, staying on MLK. They passed an elderly Black man pushing a shopping cart. Three blocks down the road, the Charger whipped to the right and stopped. Ben almost hit them.

"I think they've figured out who's following them," Ben said.

"Keep going and turn around down the road." Fitz twisted in his seat to watch. He saw two of the guys leap out of the car, grab the man pushing the shopping cart, and shove him inside. "They just grabbed another victim."

While Ben pulled into a driveway to turn the car around, Fitz watched as the Charger backed onto MLK and headed back the way it had come. "They're going back toward the shop," he said. "Give them a bit to get ahead of us before you pull out."

As soon as the Charger's tail lights were out of sight, Ben backed onto MLK and gunned the accelerator.

"Slow down or you'll give us away when we run up on them."

"Sorry," Ben said, slowing down. They saw the Charger's tail lights crossing Athens Highway. As they approached, the traffic light turned red.

"Should I run it?" Ben asked.

"No, I think we know where they're going." Fitz leaned back in the seat, and his heart sank. *If they take him to the shop, they will probably not lead us to Katía tonight.* "Let's stop at the church over there and watch the camera."

"Good idea," Ben said. When the light changed he crossed the road, pulled into the church parking lot, and opened the app on his phone. "We're in a conundrum, you know."

"Yeah, they probably won't go get Katía tonight."

"It's worse than that."

Fitz looked at Ben, wondering what he was getting at. "What do you mean?"

"If we go in and save this guy from whatever they're going to do, we risk their killing Zee and Katía since the operation is exposed. Or we can sacrifice this guy in hopes of finding Zee and Katía later."

CHAPTER 45

Fitz squirmed in his seat as the truth of Ben's comment hammered his heart. "I don't want to have to play God. Oh, no! What if I was wrong and they don't go to the shop? What if they were taking him to where they're holding Zee and Katía?"

"Any way I parse it, dreadful things happen. If they don't show, we might be able to save Katía when they bring her, but that puts Zee and this other guy at risk. If they do show, then we have to play God."

Ben's eyes were glued to the phone. Fitz joined him, every fiber of his being willing the guys not to show up.

Freddy's image flashed past the doorway. They could hear in the background, "Put the gun down. It's us."

"I hate to tell you this, but that ain't no woman," Freddy said.

"He practically jumped into the car," Gene said. "We had to accept such an eager volunteer. Take him back and get him settled." Two of the guys and the old man they had abducted passed by.

"How you gonna explain to the boss about the computer bein' gone?" they heard Ernie ask.

"I haven't figured that out yet. I guess I'll have to tell him someone broke in again."

"He ain't gonna like that."

"You got any better ideas?... I didn't think so."

"He should know before he gets here. What if they call the police to this place?"

"We have the police in our pockets, remember?"

"Still, he might want to shut the operation down."

"You sure are dumb, you know it? Think of all the money we lose if he shuts it down. The more I think about it, the more I think it's best if he don't know about the missing computer."

"Like he's not gonna notice it's gone."

"Shut up and check Walmart to see if they have one like it."

"What kind was it?"

"I don't know. Go ask Freddy. You sure are stupid."

Ben looked at Fitz. "These guys are a bunch of clowns. They could pass as the Three Stooges. Well, except that there are five of them."

"I don't think Gene is as dumb as the rest of them. But how is he going to pass off a new computer as the old one? It won't have any of the stuff on it."

"That blows your theory about his being smarter than the others. But at least he's coming up with a plan. As much as I enjoy the comedy show, we need to start making our own plans. What are we going to do?"

Ernie walked past the monitor. "Freddy says it looked like this one."

"That's five hundred dollars!" Expletives flowed while Gene fished out his wallet. Handing Ernie cash, he said, "Here. Take the car and go get that computer. If they don't have that exact one, call me."

"I really can't wait to see how this ends," Ben laughed. "If we go in while Ernie's gone, it will only be four against two."

"I'm betting if we wait long enough, the four goons will leave again. But we still have an impossible choice to make."

Heavy silence, darker than the night, settled over the car. Fitz tried to make sense of the situation. *They've killed once, I'm sure of it. If they proceed with whatever operation they're doing, they'll kill this guy when they're done. I can't let that happen.*

On the other hand, if we do something to interrupt this surgery, they could kill Zee and Katia before we find them. They wouldn't want them talking either.

Fitz was deep in thought when Ben said, "I can't sit by and let them do whatever they are going to do to this poor guy. I just can't. We have to get him out of there."

"We don't have to do anything right now. We have time to think this through and come up with a plan. Right now he's safe and sound with a nice bed."

"I don't know that I'd call it safe and sound, but you're right. He's not in any danger at the moment." Ben wrung the steering wheel with his hands.

"The goons seem willing to go to any extent to keep this operation going. They must be getting paid a lot of money."

"Yeah, I can't wait till their boss boots up the new computer and there's nothing on it. I'd love to watch that in real time."

"Help me think this through. If we break in and rescue this guy, what will the goons do? They know we're onto them, but they seem to be willing to keep going anyway." Fitz pulled on his beard.

"Remember, they plan to come hunting us once they get the place put back together. So for now they consider the operation salvageable."

"Oh, yeah. I forgot that little detail. In their minds, we'll be out of the picture by morning."

"I hope to foil that plan," Ben said.

"Do you think they would still try to salvage it if we got the guy out of there or do they give up at that point?"

"They seem very money motivated. I bet they'll let the procedure roll and hope we don't show up. They seemed sure we couldn't get law enforcement involved."

"That would be the perfect trap," Fitz tugged his beard.

"What?"

"If they can't find us tonight, they set up an ambush at the shop in the morning. They know we'll show up, so they plan to catch us then."

Ben scrunched up his forehead. "Why would they think we'll show up in the morning? They don't know that we know about the procedure."

"Good point. They don't know what we're going to do next."

"Do you think they know we're after Katía and Zee?"

"I don't know."

The heavy silence hovered again, both men trying to unravel a foggy future. After a few minutes, Fitz said, "I am sure of one thing."

"What's that?"

"If we derail their deal, they won't just let Katía and Zee go and say, 'Sorry for the inconvenience.'"

Ben met Fitz's gaze. "I'm afraid you're right. I don't like this dilemma."

They turned their attention back to Ben's phone, watching the final touches being put on the cleanup job.

Fitz said, "I wonder who the boss is."

CHAPTER 46

Max Herringer paced the study of his old, elegant home on Lullwater Road. He rattled around in the house alone, his wife having divorced him years ago before they had any children. She insisted he was really married to his work instead of her. He thought of her bitterly.

Just look at what you missed out on. Of course my work was more important than you. I'm on the brink of discovering something that will change the world. And you're living with an accountant.

Thinking of the man she had married prompted him to reach for an antacid tablet to calm the gnawing in his gut. He glanced at the clock. *It's 9:15. Why haven't they called?* Marching to his desk, he pulled out the burner phone. Gene's was the only number in it. He punched call.

"I haven't heard from you. Is everything set for in the morning?"

* * * * *

Ben pointed to the phone and turned up the volume. Gene was answering a call.

"Hey, Boss… Yeah, everything's fine. We're just getting the volunteer settled in for the night." Boomer cut his laugh short when Gene scowled and pointed his finger at him.

"Actually, we caught another one on our way to pick her up and just brought him straight here. He'll be nice and fresh for you… Got it." He disconnected.

"You lie real good," Moe said.

"Shut up," Gene retorted. "Why isn't Ernie back yet? We have to eliminate those two guys before tomorrow. I can't risk them messing things up."

Ben said, "At least we know what they're planning next. That's helpful."

"How do these guys think they can find us? They're buying a new computer and hoping the boss doesn't notice it has none of the files on it for Pete's sake." Fitz chuckled.

"Got it!" they heard Ernie call. They all gathered in the operating room.

"Turn it on," Gene ordered.

"I hate to ask a dumb question, but why won't the boss know this isn't the same computer?" Boomer asked.

"Because the computer ain't gonna work, idiot," Gene said. He pulled out a knife, took the power cord, and cut through one of the wires right at the plug. "Plug it in. Freddy, keep an eye on this thing and make sure the battery runs all the way down. When the boss tries to turn it on, it won't work."

"I have to give him credit. That's a clever plan," Ben said, rubbing his neck. "I need to shave."

"So this guy does have a couple of brain cells," Fitz observed.

"I'm not feeling so confident about their inability to find us now."

"Maybe they'll tell us how they plan to do that."

"Everybody out. Freddy, look around and make sure everything looks right."

Freddy hobbled around, holding his ribs and looking into a few drawers. "Looks good to me."

"Good. You got your gun?"

"No. They stole it when they broke in."

"Well they probably won't come back anyway. Call me if they do. OK boys, let's go spill some blood."

"How we gonna find them?" Moe asked.

"Our good friend Ron is going to give us their address."

A shockwave hit Fitz. "So it's definitely true. Ron is in on this. I had hoped I was wrong."

"That means they're going to my house. We have to get back so they don't destroy the place. And Snickers and King are there." Ben started the car.

"Hold on a minute, and let's think this through," Fitz said. "We can hurry back to your house and get in a fire fight with them… Or we could wait until they're about halfway there and break into the shop."

"How is that second option going to save my house?" Ben fretted.

"We give Freddy a chance to call. They'll come back, and we'll be gone before they get there." Fitz noted the time on his watch: 9:42.

Ben rubbed his beard again. "There's a problem with our plan."

"What's that?"

"We're not thinking about the boss. If we don't catch him or her, or whatever you call a person who would do this kind of thing, it all continues. How can we shut the whole thing down?"

"Good point. We have about five minutes to figure it out." Fitz noticed Ben lean back and close his eyes. Fitz thought better with his eyes open. He was nervous with them closed.

Ben slammed a hand on the steering wheel. "I should have thought of that earlier."

Fitz eyed him. "You care to explain?"

"We should have unlocked that garage door in the back and disengaged the opener."

"It's a little late for that, but it was a good idea."

"When we go back in, let's do that."

"When are we going back in?" Fitz asked.

"How does this sound? We give them fifteen minutes and go re-kidnap the abducted guy. Freddy calls, and the goons come back. With the victim missing, they have to go get Katía and bring her in. When the boss shows up tomorrow we break in and catch the whole crew."

Fitz pulled on his beard. "It has potential. What are the pitfalls?"

"Number one is they get spooked, call the boss, and he calls everything off. Then Katía and Zee are dead."

"That's a big pitfall. I'm also thinking that the goons won't be here for the procedure. They don't seem to know much about the place since Freddy had to tell them where to put everything." Fitz observed.

"The other pitfall is what do we do with them if we catch them? If we can't call the police, I'm not taking them home with me."

"Another good point. I think we're in a predicament."

"You can say that again." Ben said.

They fell back into pondering, each minute seeming to last half an hour. Fitz realized his heart was pounding. *I don't think I can make a decision like this. Either way, I'm sentencing someone to death.*

CHAPTER 47

A bead of sweat rolled down Fitz's forehead. His pounding heart got louder. He expected Ben to say something about the sound. He searched his mind for a workable solution to their problem.

Suddenly, Ben cranked the car and pulled into the shadow of the church. "They're leaving and, I bet, heading this way," Ben explained. "We have to figure something out quick."

"I just can't make this call. Let's go defend your house."

They watched as the Charger rolled by and stopped at the traffic light. "I hope we're in the shadows enough," Fitz whispered.

The light turned green, and the Charger crossed Highway 129, turned right onto Athens Street, and right again into the Burger King parking lot.

"Someone must be hungry," Ben noted.

"Either that, or they spotted us and are turning around."

Ben reached to crank the car. "Wait," Fitz said. "Let's see what they do." The gang parked and went into the restaurant.

"I can see them, so they can still see us. Can you start the car without pressing the brakes?"

"No."

"Great. I guess we have to hope they don't notice. Let's go."

Ben started the car then rolled out of the parking lot and took a left onto MLK, making sure not to tap the brakes or turn on the lights. Once they were out of sight of the restaurant, he turned on the lights and took a right onto Bradford Street.

"Let's get to your house before they do," Fitz urged.

"That's where I'm headed, but what are we going to do if they show up?"

"They'll show up. We've made them mad, and Ron will give them your address. I guess the best thing to do would be to turn off all the lights and hope they drive on by, assuming you're not there."

"I think they'll notice your car sitting out front."

"True, but I can move it."

"Wouldn't it be better to lure them in and try to capture them? Then we could learn where they're holding Zee and Katía."

Fitz eyed Ben, weighing his next question. "Do you know how to shoot a gun?"

"Yes, I know how to do that."

"I get the feeling you know more about this kind of thing than you're letting on. Let me guess, military training?"

"Yeah. I was part of Special Ops with the Green Beret. I mostly did the computer stuff, but had to know the rest, too."

"That explains a lot."

"It's been a while, though."

"That's true. Let's not get into any hand-to-hand stuff, then. I know one of them has a gun, and they know I have one. With both of us armed, we should have the element of surprise."

"I think they'll be expecting us to be there," Ben noted.

"I mean they don't expect you to have a gun, too… at least I hope."

Ben hit the garage door opener and pulled in the car. "I need to let the dogs out before they get here," he said, hurrying into the house. He stopped and stood up straight. "This isn't right. If we ambush them, they'll know we knew they were coming. They'll figure out the camera is there."

"Do you really think they're that smart?"

"I'd bet Gene is." Ben rubbed his hand over his thinning hair.

"So what do we do? Act like they surprised us?"

"That's too dangerous. Plus, I don't want to kill anyone tonight. Let's grab the dogs and get out of here," Ben said.

"I don't know. I'd really like to at least put some rat shot in those guys."

Ben paused. "That's tempting, but I still think it's dangerous. I don't want to get shot through my own window." He hurried into the house and opened the back door. Snickers and King ran out. "Hurry," he advised.

Fitz battled his nerves while he waited for the dogs to return. He had never been one to run from a fight. He didn't want to run now but had to admit that Ben made sense. With Ben standing at the back door waiting for the dogs, he tried to find a plan that felt right.

That's when he noticed dark movement out the dining room window. "They're here. Take cover," he said just loudly enough for Ben to hear. "Remember, your first bullet is rat shot. It won't kill anybody."

A hunch sent Fitz out the door into the garage. The garage door was still open. While closing the door into the house, he glanced and saw Ben slip out the back. Their eyes met. Ben pointed, indicating he was going around the end of the house opposite the garage. The dogs started barking as soon as they were back inside.

Fitz moved to the edge of the garage door and peeked around. "It's him," one of the guys called.

Hearing footsteps hurrying toward him, Fitz stepped out and raised his gun. "You guys come for coffee?"

It was Boomer headed his way, crowbar in hand. He hit the brakes and started backpedaling when he saw Fitz's gun aimed at his heart. He crashed into Moe, who was right behind him, and tripped and fell.

"Get off me," Moe yelled then aimed a handgun at Fitz.

"You're way too slow," Fitz said as he fired, hitting Moe in the thigh with the rat shot.

Moe dropped his gun, grabbed his thigh, and landed on top of Boomer wailing. Gene poked his head around the corner, saw the two guys on the ground, and yelled, "Let's get out of here!" He and Ernie ran toward the Charger, which was parked three houses down.

Fitz chuckled as Boomer shoved Moe off him and got up to run. "You guys really are the four stooges."

A shot rang out as Boomer crossed the yard, prompting him to double his speed. Moe struggled to his feet.

"You want me to call an ambulance?" Fitz asked.

"No, I'm good," Moe answered and started limping toward the car as fast as he could. "Wait for me," he yelled as the car engine came to life.

Fitz heard Ben laughing before they met at the front door. "These guys really should go on the road as a comedy team," Ben said.

"You missed the one you shot at," Fitz noted.

"I was just trying to motivate him to run a little faster."

"Your friends are going to pay for this," Gene called from the car. "An eye for an eye."

"I shouldn't have missed," Ben said.

Fitz walked back and picked up the handgun Moe had dropped. "It's a Glock. You want it?"

"No, but I'll hang onto it till we find some credible law enforcement. Let me get a zip lock bag." They went back into the house, the gun dangling from Fitz's hand by the barrel.

"Do you think they're serious about hurting Katía and Zee?" Ben asked.

"Yeah. Dead serious."

CHAPTER 48

itz crawled onto one of Ben's barstools and rested his head in his hands. "I'm getting too old for this."

"Tell me about it," Ben replied, sliding onto the other stool. "But we can't stop now. I'll make some more coffee." He hopped back up. "What do you think they'll do to them?"

"I don't know. I don't think they'll kill them, though. An eye for an eye suggests Gene was thinking something proportional."

"I'm tired of feeling helpless. I wish we had killed all of them."

"No you don't," Fitz said.

The look Ben gave him led Fitz to believe he was serious. "Maybe that would have been a relief, but they might be the only ones who know where Katía and Zee are."

"True. So can we make the goons suffer once we find them?"

Fitz laughed. "Sure. But what are we going to do now?" Ben slid onto the stool next to him, and they watched the coffee dripping into the pot. The soothing aroma worked its way over to them.

Weird. It's been a long time since I've had any M&Ms. He reached into his pocket and pulled out a few. "Want some?" he asked.

"No, thanks," Ben replied. "Since we don't know where they're going, we need to do something to draw them back to us before they hurt our friends. But what could we do?"

Fitz sat up straight. "That's it!"

"What's it?"

"We go back to the first plan. If we snatch the guy from the shop, they'll either come to see what happened or bring Katía so the boss will have a victim."

"Remember the caveat where they tell the boss what's going on, call off the whole business, and kill the remaining captives?" Ben observed.

"Oh, yeah. That is a risk. We need to get into these guys heads a little better."

The silence resumed. The coffee stopped dripping. "I hate no-win situations," Fitz grumbled. He popped some more M&Ms into his mouth.

"Stress getting to you?"

"It looks like it."

"Me, too. I'd feel better if we had a plan." He got up and poured two thermoses of coffee. "Black, right?"

"Oh, yeah. Wouldn't have it any other way," Fitz answered.

"I can't see any way out of this without someone dying," Ben said. "So I guess we need to pick the path of least destruction."

Fitz's eyes lit up when the idea struck. "Ben, you're a genius. Someone does have to die, and that's our ticket. Let's go. I'll explain on the way. Got any zip-ties?"

Ben parked in the lot behind the shop, making sure the car was in darkness. Fitz set his phone to silent after punching send on the last of the texts he needed to deliver. It was 2:18 in the morning. Clouds covered the sky, leaving the area surprisingly well-lit from reflected city light.

"Let's do this," Fitz said.

They slipped out of the car and made their way to the front door of the shop. With Ben holding a light, Fitz picked the lock as quietly as he could. He stood to the side while Ben pulled the door open, cringing at the squeak of the hinges.

He stuck a hand through the doorway and quickly pulled it back. Next he poked his head through. Freddy was nowhere to be seen. Motioning to Ben, he entered the building, and Ben closed the door behind them.

They heard music coming from the back. Fitz smiled, and they pushed farther inside. They found Freddy sound asleep with his music playing.

"That was easier than anticipated," Fitz whispered. "You do the honors of waking sleeping beauty."

Ben yanked Freddy up by the collar and pressed his gun to his temple. "Don't move and please don't sing."

Freddy groaned and grabbed his ribs, eyes failing to focus.

"He's loopy on pain medication," Fitz laughed. "Perfect." He stepped close to Freddy and asked. "Are you awake?"

Freddy nodded.

"Good. We have a problem. The guy they brought in earlier is dead. I assume you killed him?"

Freddy shook his head hard enough to make him groan.

"That's what I'm going to tell Gene unless you have a better solution." Fitz pulled his phone from his pocket, pretending to dial.

"No. Wait," Freddy pleaded.

"I'm sure Gene won't mind that you killed a subject. They're a dime a dozen, right? You've already killed at least one."

"That wasn't me. That was Gene and his cronies. I haven't killed anyone. I just help in the lab. That's all." Freddy's words were a bit slurred but intelligible enough.

"Freddy, you seem like a decent soul. I'm going to give you a break. Why don't you call Gene and tell him the guy died of a heart attack, just keeled over and you found him dead?"

Freddy shook his head.

"OK, if you insist." Fitz started punching numbers into his phone.

"Wait," Freddy said. "Is he really dead?"

"Yep. We just found him. He's already stiff." Ben affirmed. "It looks like a crowbar to the head to me."

"Gene needs to know what you've done. I'm not waiting any longer," Fitz said.

"OK. OK. I'll tell him he died of a heart attack."

"And when he fell off the bed, he hit his head," Ben prompted.

"Yeah. Yeah. That makes sense. I don't remember hurting him, though."

"I think you went too heavy on the pain medicine," Ben coaxed.

"Since you're so stoned, we went ahead and wrote out what to say. Just read this, and Gene will believe it was a heart attack."

Freddy scrunched his eyes around till he was able to focus on the words.

"I don't think he can read," Ben said. "I guess we're going to have to tell Gene the truth."

"I can read. I just can't get my eyes to focus."

"You've got about fifteen seconds to fix that," Fitz said. "One… two… three…"

"OK. I see it. Where's my phone?"

"Here you go. It was right beside you," Ben said, holding out the phone he had snitched earlier. "This guy's worthless. Can we just shoot him for killing the other guy and be done with it?"

"No! Don't do that!" Freddy lunged for his phone, the sharp pain in his ribs prompting another groan.

"Call Gene and read exactly what's on the paper, or Ben will have his way with you," Fitz growled.

While Freddy tapped the phone to dial Gene, Ben held his gun to his head. "Put it on speaker."

After Freddy hung up, Fitz said, "Bravo! A command performance." He held out his hand. "Phone, please." Stuffing Freddy's phone into his pocket he asked, "Now, how do we get to the back of the shop where the garage door is?"

"There's a garage door?" Freddy asked, eyes crossing slightly.

"Can anyone really be that dumb?" Ben asked.

Fitz looked around, realizing the place was set up with cubicle partitions. "It should be diagonally across from the front door. We need to find a break in the partitions. Watch him and I'll hunt."

Entering the last room on the right, he found a break in the corner and was able to push the partitions apart far enough to get through. The space behind was empty.

"Bring him on," Fitz called.

"After you," Ben said, directing Freddy to move toward Fitz's voice.

"Zip-ties, please," Fitz said as Ben led Freddy to the back corner next to the garage door. Fitz zip-tied Freddy's ankles together. "If you'll promise to behave, I'll leave your hands free since your ribs are broken."

"I promise."

"Do you trust his mouth?" Ben asked.

"Of course not. Find something to gag him."

Ben came back dragging a mattress.

"I don't think his mouth is that big," Fitz quipped.

"No, but the blanket will work. He's been such a model citizen, I think he deserves a mattress."

As Fitz was cutting a strip off the blanket to gag Freddy, Ben walked in leading the guy they had abducted.

Freddy's eyes popped wide, like he was seeing a ghost. "He's not dead?"

"It doesn't look like it, does it?" Ben said.

"This will all be over soon, and you can get those ribs checked out," Fitz said as he tied the gag.

Ben disappeared, and Fitz said, "Hi, I'm Fitz."

"Joseph," the Black man said. "What exactly is going on here?"

"It appears you were abducted as part of an illegal medical experiment."

"You mean like the Tuskegee thing?"

"Sort of, but this one is being done by one really evil doctor. If you don't mind, we're going to need you to wait here till we wrap up this case."

Ben walked in dragging another mattress. "This should make the wait a little more comfortable."

CHAPTER 49

Joseph followed Fitz and Ben back into the lab area. "What were they going to do to me?"

"We think it was some kind of brain surgery," Ben answered. "Do you need to call family and tell them you're OK?"

"Nah. I live on the street. Got nobody to call. They did leave my buggy behind when they grabbed me, though."

"We don't have time to go after it now," Fitz said. "Maybe it'll still be there in the morning."

"I hope so. It's got all my worldly goods."

"They seem to be especially talented at nabbing homeless folks," Ben noted. "As far as I know, Katía's the only one they've abducted who doesn't live on the streets."

"They thought she was homeless when they grabbed her," Fitz reminded him.

"Oh, yeah. It's been so long I'd forgotten that."

"Are they only grabbing Black folk?" Joseph asked.

"As far as we can tell," Fitz answered.

"This is one sick world," Joseph groaned.

"That's true," Fitz said, "And the four sickos who abducted you will be walking through the front door soon with another victim. I need you to be in the back where you're safe and out of the way."

"I'll be happy to help," Joseph said.

"The thing we need the most help with is making sure that other guy doesn't try to sneak out the back. Would you keep an eye on him?"

"Sure, I can do that." Joseph moseyed to the back. Fitz and Ben heard, "You'd better stay on that mattress, or I'll knock you into next week."

"I think he's in good hands," Ben chuckled. "Do you have a plan for taking the next crew?"

"Yeah. The first part involves managing to stay awake till they get here," Fitz yawned. "We have to make sure they all get inside then stop anyone from getting out."

"All while not getting Katía hurt or getting shot ourselves. This should be a cinch. I wonder how long it will take them to get here?"

Fitz glanced at his watch, which read 3:47. "If they're true to their word, about forty more minutes."

"Why don't you grab a nap and I'll wake you in twenty-five minutes? You could use some beauty sleep."

"Thanks for the compliment. I think I'd better stay awake. I don't want to be groggy when our guests arrive."

They sat down in chairs in the hallway. Fitz leaned his head back against the wall. "Remember we don't have any more rat shot. The next bullets kill." He looked over, and Ben's eyes were closed. *I think I'll rest my eyes a minute, too.*

The next thing Fitz knew, he heard the front door opening and Gene yelling, "Freddy, how could you let that guy die of a heart attack?"

Fitz jumped to his feet, startling Ben. He held his fingers to his lips and pointed toward the front of the building. Ben was on his feet, too, gun in hand. Fitz gestured to the room next to them. Ben slipped inside it, and Fitz crossed the hall to hide in the room where Joseph had been.

"Freddy, get in here. We have the next volunteer. Moe and Ernie, get her settled in a room. Boomer, find Freddy. He must be asleep." Gene's voice got louder as they came closer.

"You be a good little girl and come with me," Ernie said.

When they were all in the hallway, Fitz stepped out. "Welcome. I'm glad you could join us. If you will, be a good boy and drop your gun, Gene."

Gene hesitated. Fitz could tell he was weighing his options.

"Put it on the floor nice and slow," Fitz directed.

Gene glanced at Ernie, then put his gun on the floor. A sudden commotion caught Fitz's attention.

"Drop your weapon or I slice her throat." Ernie was behind Katía with a knife to her neck.

"Nobody needs to get hurt here. Let her go," Fitz said.

"You're the one who decides if anyone gets hurt," Gene snapped.

Ben slipped out of the room, pushed the barrel of his gun against Ernie's temple, and said, "You might want to rethink this. You have till three. One. Two."

Ernie moved the knife away from Katía's neck.

"Drop it," Ben ordered.

Ernie let the knife drop to the floor, and Moe lunged for it. In a fluid motion, Ben put his foot on the knife, slid it away, and slammed Ernie on top of Moe.

"You guys never cease to amaze me," Ben said. "You OK, Katía?"

"I've been better," she replied.

Fitz looked back to Gene to see him opening his phone. Without a word, he fired, blasting the phone out of Gene's hand. "Naughty, naughty," Fitz said. "The next one goes in your heart. We have a nice party planned for you guys. Please make your way to the back of the building."

The four goons marched to the back and through the gap in the partitions. "Find a place to make yourself comfortable," Ben told Katía as he followed Fitz to the back.

Boomer made a break for the garage door and tried to pull it open.

"Do you honestly think I won't shoot you?" Fitz asked. "Everyone face down on the floor. Will you do the honors, Ben?"

"Gladly."

"I'll be happy to help," Joseph said, getting up from the other side of the room. They proceeded to zip-tie four sets of ankles and wrists.

"Aren't you glad you cooperated and everything is so nice and cozy? I think we're going to have a swell time," Ben quipped.

"You're going to pay for this. I have friends in high places. You just wait and see."

"That's scary," Fitz said, pretending to shiver. "We have plans for your good friend, Ron, too. Don't expect him to get you out of this." He looked around, puzzled. "What is that noise?"

"That guy passed out, and I don't think he's breathing too good," Joseph said, referring to Freddy.

"I'll relieve him of his gag for now," Ben offered. He removed the gag. Freddie didn't budge, but the snoring quietened. "I'm checking on Katía. Keep an eye on them." Ben rushed out of the room.

Fitz watched them while listening in on the conversation. "What have they done to you?" he heard Ben ask.

"They've had us chained to beds in a house with no electricity."

"Was Zee with you?"

"Yeah, poor guy. He couldn't even remember how long he'd been held captive. What is this place?"

"It seems to be some sort of medical experimentation place. The doctor is coming in the morning to do surgery on you."

"In that case, I'm leaving."

"Your best bet is to stay right here till we catch this guy. Who knows what's lurking out there this time of night? Besides, it will be quite a show in the morning."

CHAPTER 50

Katía guarded the goons while Fitz and Ben slept for an hour and a half. Fitz's alarm jolted him awake at 7:30am. He walked to the back. "Everything OK?"

"Yeah. I was afraid I was going to have to clip a few kneecaps, but they settled down."

Freddy was awake and leaning against the wall. "Feeling better?" Fitz asked.

"No. I need more pain medicine."

"You enjoy that a little too much. It'll have to wait."

Ben stretched and groaned just inside the back room. "It's going to be a glorious day. We get to meet the boss, and all of you get to go to jail. Life is good, isn't it?"

His comment drew angry glares. He just grinned in return.

"You're enjoying this," Fitz observed.

"I haven't had this much excitement in a long time."

Katía shook her head. "Good grief."

"Does anyone care to tell us if the doctor shows up alone?" Fitz asked.

"I'll tell if you bring me more pain medicine," Freddy said.

"Shut up, Freddy," Gene barked. "We ain't tellin' this guy nothin'."

"Suit yourself," Fitz said and started to leave.

"Wait," Freddy called. "I'm hurting. I need medicine."

Fitz turned around. "I'm a man of my word. If you tell me, I'll bring you a pain pill."

"I took three last time."

"And look where it got you. One is enough."

"OK. He comes alone."

"You're going to pay for that." Gene started scooting toward Freddy.

Ben walked over and smashed his foot into Gene's face, knocking him flat on his back. "I don't think so."

"Are you telling the truth?" Fitz asked.

"Yeah," Freddy said.

Fitz disappeared and returned with a pain pill and a cup of water. Freddy swallowed it greedily.

"How come his hands ain't tied like ours?" Boomer asked.

"Because he's a better man than you," Fitz said. He checked his watch: 7:49. "Let's get these canaries gagged."

With the five men gagged, Ben looked to Fitz. "We only have two guns. I think we need both of them up front just in case."

"True," Fitz answered. "We have the knife… Freddy's the only one that poses a risk, and he can't walk… We need a heavy stick of some kind."

"How about a chair?" Ben asked. "If Freddy gets up, Katía can clobber him with it."

Ben dragged one of the chairs from the hall back to Katía. "Use this if he gets up."

"Gladly." She picked up the chair. "Nice and sturdy. It'll break some bones." She flashed a smile at Freddy.

"I won't get up. I promise," he said, scooting a little farther away from Katía.

Fitz and Ben positioned themselves in the operating room to wait. Ben sat on the table, and Fitz took the chair. Hopping off the table, Ben said, "We've overlooked one detail."

"What's that?"

"I need another pain pill. Where did you find them?"

Fitz pointed to the drawer. "Do you care to explain?"

"We don't know if Freddy usually leaves the door locked or unlocked for the good doctor."

"Good point."

Ben headed to the back with the pain pill. Holding it so Freddy could see, he asked, "Do you have the door locked when the doctor comes?" Freddy nodded his head. He handed him the pill and undid the gag long enough for him to swallow it.

It was precisely 8:45am when Ben and Fitz heard the lock turning. The door opened and closed. "Good morning," a cheerful voice called. "I think today is the day. Everything is going to go perfectly."

"I think you're right," Fitz said, stepping into the front room and leveling his gun at Dr. Max Herringer's heart. "You're right on time."

"What's going on? Who are you?" Herringer stammered.

"We're the team putting an end to your despicable practice," Ben said as he stepped into the room, his gun also leveled at Herringer's heart.

Herringer's eyes darted around the room. He eased toward the door.

"Don't even think about it. You've killed at least one person, so I don't have any qualms about returning the favor," Fitz said.

"I haven't killed anyone," Herringer stated.

"No, but your buddies did at your request," Fitz returned.

Herringer looked like a trapped raccoon, flitting his eyes everywhere trying to come up with a way to escape.

"Come on back and join the party. We have about twenty-five minutes to wait," Ben directed.

Herringer moved toward the back of the building. He bolted into the operating room and turned toward Ben, scalpel in hand.

"Cute," Ben said. "Can I shoot him now?"

"Hold on, Ben. We want him to get his full reward."

Herringer drew back and threw the scalpel. Ben dodged, and it embedded in the wall just beyond his head. In the blink of an eye, another scalpel flew. Fitz moved just in time, and it only grazed his left arm, leaving a thin line of blood in its wake.

When Herringer drew back with a third scalpel, Ben fired, hitting him in the shoulder. Herringer careened backwards, crashing into the counter and then falling to the floor.

"Had enough?" Fitz asked.

Herringer rocked on the floor, holding the injured shoulder. Fitz noticed a light in Herringer's injured hand and realized he was trying to place a call.

Fitz stepped down on his fingers, hearing a crack. "Oops."

"I'm a surgeon, you fool."

"Not anymore," Fitz said, prying the phone from his hand.

"I don't know, they might let surgeons practice in prison," Ben quipped.

Fitz laughed. "That would be mutual punishment. I like it."

"You will pay for attacking me. I have people on the way to put an end to this insult."

"You can say that again," Ben laughed. "You just lie right there and maybe you won't bleed to death before your big show."

CHAPTER 51

At 9:15am, Fitz said to Ben, "Look outside and see if they're here."

Ben opened the door and looked out. His jaw dropped. "Man are they here! You're not going to believe this!" he called back to Fitz.

"What do you mean?"

"You'll see. Let's start the parade." While Ben walked to the back, Fitz placed a 911 call. "I need two ambulances… One is a gunshot victim, and I think the other broke some ribs… I don't know the address, but I'm on Martin Luther King, Jr. Boulevard in an abandoned shop. Just locate my phone… I don't have time for that now. I'll leave the phone connected."

Turning to Herringer, he said, "See, I wasn't just going to let you lie there and die even though I should have. It's show time. Up on your feet."

Herringer groaned as Fitz pulled him to his feet. They watched as Joseph led the way with Boomer, Moe, Ernie, Gene, and Freddy following.

"I see you've got your ducks in a row," Fitz said as Katía and Ben brought up the rear.

"You know it," Ben smiled. "The look on the good doctor's face is priceless. I wish we had time for a picture. Are these the guys you were counting on to do us in?" he directed to Herringer. "I say we save the main attraction for last."

"That's only fitting," Fitz said. He grabbed the collar of Herringer's jacket and shoved him forward, falling in line behind the others. "Let's see what's waiting outside."

The sun was shining brightly, and Fitz squinted as he pushed Herringer out the door. As his eyes adjusted, his jaw dropped. Hundreds of people filled the parking lot and lined the street. A few hundred feet away, patrol cars had the street blocked.

"Where did all these people come from?" Fitz whispered to Ben.

"I might have sent a couple of texts."

"A couple?"

"Yeah, to Luna and the Newtown Florist Club."

Fitz returned Ben's grin. Serena, Mayor Thompson, Chief of Police Arnold, Sheriff Tucker, and Luna stepped out of the crowd. Fitz spotted a cameraman moving around to the left as the sounds of ambulance sirens blared a few blocks away.

Mayor Thompson asked, "Who's in charge here?" Ben and Katía pointed to Fitz and Fitz pointed to Herringer.

Then Fitz grinned. "I guess it depends on what kind of 'in charge' you're asking about. This guy," he gave Herringer a shake, "has been conducting illegal surgeries on African Americans. I'm fairly certain he is responsible for the corpse discovered a few days ago at the industrial site. The vermin wearing zip-ties are his lackeys."

The ambulance sirens ceased as officers helped them work their way through the crowd. Fitz glanced toward the ambulances, and something suspicious caught his eye. He did a double take and realized it was Ron Carson talking with one of the officers.

Fitz's smile grew. "This is our lucky day." He flicked his eyes toward Carson so Ben would notice. Then he whispered to the sheriff, "One of your deputies, Ron Carson, has been assisting this crew by covering up their operation. He's talking to the officer over there."

Without hesitation, Sheriff Tucker said to a nearby policeman, "Communicate with that officer to arrest Ron Carson, please."

Fitz watched as Ron bolted when the radioed message came through. Two officers chased him down and handcuffed him. Fitz could tell they were reading him his rights.

"Those are mighty big claims," Mayor Thompson said. "I hope you have proof."

Ben pulled up some of the video footage from the camera they had installed. The five people leaned in to watch. Even Herringer seemed interested.

After the footage played for a couple of minutes, Chief Arnold said, "That's enough evidence for me. Officer Wirth, we need enough cars to haul in," he paused while counting, "seven less two, five men to jail and two officers to accompany the two going to the hospital."

Officer Wirth counted the cars on site and called for one more as well as two officers to go to the hospital. While he was counting, the two officers dragged Ron up, one holding each arm.

"You know, I never really trusted you," Sheriff Tucker said. "Take him in and book him."

"Wirth, while you're at it, we're going to need detectives and enough folks to process this crime scene. I think it's going to be all hands on deck," Chief Arnold barked.

"They're on their way," Wirth called back.

Fitz leaned in and whispered to Chief Arnold, "I think the guy with the broken ribs will be cooperative with the investigation."

"Thanks. That's good to know. Wirth?"

"Yes, sir?"

"Tell whoever goes with the broken ribs guy to be nice to him."

"Yes, sir." Wirth went off to fulfill his orders.

Serena asked, "Chief, do you have a statement for the press?"

"I'll get with you on that after a while. This is a lot to process, and right now I have to check out this crime scene."

A man came charging out of the crowd yelling, "You! You!" His fist was cocked and aimed right at Herringer's face. Ben stepped in, whipped the arm around the man's back, and had him by both elbows.

"I can't believe I actually wanted to work with you! You're the scum of the earth!"

"That's true," Ben said. "But I need you to calm down."

"And who are you? Chief Arnold asked.

"I'm Dr. Stan Cole."

"He's going to get what he deserves. Will you behave if I let you go now?" Ben asked.

"Yes. Sorry about that. I lost my cool. I had offered to help this goat with his clinical trials. I'm thankful that didn't happen," Stan said, staring a hole through Herringer.

The sneer on Herringer's face unsettled Fitz. *Does he have something else planned?*

As the criminals were tucked away into police cars, the crowd lining the street and parking lot broke into applause.

"Let's have a look inside," Chief Arnold said.

Fitz slapped himself on the forehead. "Why didn't I think of that earlier!"

"Think of what?" Ben asked.

"Zee's in Lula, isn't he Katía?"

"I think that's where we were," she answered.

"Pull up that house we went to. Don't you see? They found the same place we had just searched. They got there right after we left."

"That explains why we saw them leaving Lula." Ben searched his phone for the address till he found it. He started to hand it to the sheriff then stopped. "We don't know how many corrupt deputies you have. Chief, do you have an officer you can trust?"

"I trust Wirth. He's never given me any reason not to."

"There's another captive in Lula. We need to get him into safe hands."

Chief Arnold called Officer Wirth over and said, "There's another hostage in Lula. I need for you to get him picked up."

"I'll get on it, sir. Could I have the address?"

Ben showed him his phone, and Wirth copied down the address. Ben caught up with Katía just before they went inside. "How are you holding up?"

"I have to admit I'm rattled. This has been an ordeal. I'll be glad when Zee gets here. So you think they were going to do some kind of brain surgery on me?"

"That's what had happened to the dead man they found. I'm betting the surgery happened here."

"That's creepy. I can't wait to be home."

The officials followed inside and listened as Fitz showed them around and explained what had happened.

Chief Arnold spied the scalpels stuck into the wall. "I bet these have a story to tell."

One of the officers pulled out a large bag. It was filled with fentanyl. "There's enough here to kill half of the city," she said.

"I wonder if that's how they killed the man whose body was found at the industrial site," Fitz added.

"The autopsy did indicate he died of a fentanyl overdose," Sherriff Tucker said. "We had concluded the death was from his own drug use."

They were still going through things in the operating room and cataloguing the anesthesia, equipment, pain medicine, bandages, and all the other items when Chief Arnold's phone rang.

"Sorry, I need to take this," he said and stepped away. "What!" he shouted. "No way. OK, send it over."

Concern rammed Fitz's heart. *It has to be Zee.*

CHAPTER 52

Chief Arnold opened a message with a video the office had just sent over. The narrowing of Arnold's eyes sent a shock of concern through Fitz. He couldn't help asking, "What is it, Chief?"

Arnold looked up with worry on his brow. "We have a problem. Another gang member got to the captive before we did. You need to see this." He turned the phone around and restarted the video.

Zee was the only one on the screen. He held a piece of paper that said, "RELEASE THEM OR I DIE." Finally the silence was broken with a voice saying, "You took some friends of mine into custody this morning. If you want this man to live, you will release them. You have till three this afternoon." The screen went blank.

Fitz started pushing through people, moving toward the door. "It looks like they're at that house. We have to hurry." Ben, Katía, and Luna raced after him.

"Where do you think you're going? We need you for questioning," Chief Arnold called.

"That'll have to wait," Fitz answered.

Pushing out the door, he saw Wirth standing nearby. He grabbed the front of his shirt. "What did you do?"

Wirth's eyes narrowed, but he said calmly, "What do you mean?"

"You were supposed to go get Zee. Now he's being held hostage. What did you do?" Fitz's voice escalated with each word.

Wirth's eyes widened. "I called a deputy friend to go get him. I thought I'd be needed here."

"Put out an arrest warrant for that friend of yours." Fitz gave Wirth a push then hurried toward Ben's car.

The four park pals hopped into the car, and Ben tossed his phone into Fitz's lap. "Map it," he said. As fast as traffic would allow, he drove to the house in Lula.

Fitz's forearm bumped into an odd lump in his coat pocket. "I forgot all about this. Fishing Gene's gun out of his pocket, he handed it to Katía. "You might need this."

They hurried to the front door, positioning themselves with two on each side. Fitz listened but heard nothing. The knob turned when he twisted it. He flung open the door and charged in with the other three behind him.

Rushing from room to room, disappointment zeroed in on Fitz's heart. He suddenly knew they wouldn't find Zee. "He's not here. Where could they have taken him?"

"Great. Here we go again. I was looking forward to a long nap," Ben moaned.

"Katía, do you remember them saying anything about a headquarters or hideout?" Fitz asked.

She thought over the question. "One of the guys talked about taking me home with him." She shuddered at the thought. "He said he had a nice room he could keep me in, but he never said where this place was."

"Let me get this picture straight in my head," Luna said. "We don't know who we're looking for, what kind of car they drive, or where they might be. That doesn't sound very promising. I think our best bet is to try to get the police to release the goons."

"They won't do it," Fitz said. "We have until three o'clock to find Zee. That's less than five hours." He started pacing and pulling on his beard. "Where would I hold a hostage if I were part of the Confederate Rising gang? They probably have some kind of headquarters. Somebody look that up. They knew where Zee was and that we'd be coming for him, so they moved him. I'm sure it was the deputy who tipped them off. It has to be Confederate Rising. Maybe Gene isn't the leader. Any luck finding the headquarters?"

"That was quite the soliloquy," Ben quipped. "No, I didn't find anything about them except for a description of the gang and their mission."

"How about Facebook? Or X?" Katía suggested.

"I'll check," Luna said.

Fitz resumed pacing but kept his eyes on Luna. He popped M&Ms into his mouth. Time seemed crippled, barely limping as she tapped on her phone. His heart quickened when Luna's eyes narrowed. She was reading intently.

"I might have something. It's indirect but listen to this. 'When problems arise, solutions have to be found.' That one is followed by, 'The bait is laid to secure my birds' release.'" She looked up. "What do you think?"

"I think you definitely have something," Fitz said. "When were those posted?"

"Within the last ten minutes."

"It doesn't help us with where he might be, though," Ben observed. "Is there a profile picture?"

"It's the Confederate flag," Luna answered. Her phone dinged. "There's another one. It says, 'Hanging out in my lair till the appointed hour. Come join me in the watch party. I'll leave the light on for you!'"

Fitz straightened his spine when the realization hit. "They're at Motel Six. Let's go!"

"We'll have to thank that guy for his tweet," Ben said.

After speeding back to Gainesville, Ben pulled into the Motel 6 parking lot nonchalantly. "I hope this guy doesn't know what we look like," he said.

"We don't know what he looks like either, but I bet he has a Confederate flag tattoo on his neck," Fitz replied.

"That's a lot of rooms, guys," Katía observed. "Are we going to knock on every door?"

"It might be easier to ask the front desk if our friend with the tattoo checked in," Ben suggested.

"Good idea," Fitz said. "Let's go."

They walked into the lobby, and the first thing Fitz saw was a Confederate flag on the neck of the man behind the counter. He revised the plan as he approached. "Do you have a room with two queen beds?" he asked.

"No, but we have one with two full beds," the clerk said.

"That'll have to do," Fitz answered.

"I'll need a credit card. It's eighty-six dollars."

Fitz looked around, and Ben pulled out his wallet. "Here you go," he said, handing over the card.

"No judgement, but who's with who?" The clerk grinned.

"We like to mix it up," Katía said with a smile.

"Well, OK then," the clerk said, handing over the key. "If you're out by five, I won't charge you for the second day."

"Thanks," Fitz said. They left to find their room.

As soon as the door shut, Luna said, "Great. He thinks we're here for an orgy. I hope my husband doesn't hear about this."

"I'll never tell," Ben said with a grin. "Seriously, now what do we do?"

CHAPTER 53

Fitz slid the drape back and looked out the window. "This isn't exactly what I had in mind. We can't see anything from here."

"Yeah. We'd be better off in the car," Ben replied.

Katía picked up the ice bucket. "I'm going for ice."

"Ice?" Ben scrunched up his face.

"Good idea and maybe get lost on the way," Fitz said. "Just be careful."

"Why is getting ice a good idea?" Ben asked.

"It gives us a chance to look around," Luna answered. "I'm coming with you."

The women left, leaving Fitz and Ben in the room. Katía turned along the exterior corridor in the opposite direction of the ice machine. "After all of this, I might need to find a church," Luna said.

"You're welcome to come to mine. We'd love to have you."

"Maybe we'll do that if I can talk Carlos into coming. Are you married?"

"Nope. I haven't found anyone close to being the right one yet."

"I don't think you'll find him here," Luna chuckled.

"I totally agree." They reached the end of the floor and found a stairwell. "Let's go down and walk back along the next floor."

"How did you and Carlos meet?" Katía asked as they came out onto the first floor walkway.

"In college like a lot of folks. He was in physical therapy school, and I was studying to be a teacher. We graduated the same year, got married, and that was that."

"Are you happy?"

"Yes. He's a good man, and we have fun together. I highly recommend it."

They made it to the small room that housed the ice machine. A man was in there. Katía froze when she noticed the Confederate flag on his neck. Panic rose with the bile from her gut.

Luna took the ice bucket without a word. The guy noticed them waiting for him to finish and grinned. "Hey, gorgeous. You lookin' for some action?" He ogled Luna from head to toe.

"Maybe. I have to finish the old guy I came with first. I don't think he's going to have much pep," she answered.

The guys eyes lit up. "Well, come and find me. I'll be waiting."

"What room are you in?"

"One eighteen. Don't bring your friend. I don't want nothin' to do with a Black girl."

"Got it," Luna said.

The guy left with his ice bucket, and Katía pushed against the wall as he passed by. She watched him all the way to his room. She looked back to Luna just as he turned to the door.

"That was icky!" Luna said.

"You were brilliant. I hope he's the one who has Zee," Katía answered, recovering from her panic.

Luna filled the ice bucket, and they walked back to the room, trying not to hurry.

"I think we found him," Katía said when they had shut the door. "Luna has a date with him when we're done here."

"Yuk! You're going to make me vomit," Luna responded.

"That's great!" Ben said. "Let's go."

"Hold on a minute. We need a plan," Fitz said. "We have to assume he is armed, and I doubt he'll just open the door if we knock."

"Like Katía said, I have a… an appointment. But we have to wait a while to make it look legitimate."

"I hate waiting," Ben groaned.

"What exactly was the deal?" Fitz asked.

"I told him I'd come to him when I was done with you," Luna said, going red in the face.

"I see." Fitz blushed, too. "Do we know if he's alone?"

"We didn't ask. He did say he didn't want anything to do with Black girls like me," Katía said.

"OK. If he's alone, he probably has Zee cuffed to a bed, so he won't be able to help once we're inside. If you go in alone, the door will be locked, and we couldn't get in," Fitz stated.

"I'm not going in there by myself," Luna said, crossing her arms and stomping her foot.

Fitz looked Ben over, "Which one of us is in the best shape? We need to crash the door and take him down before he can get it closed."

"Actually, it's probably me," Katía said.

Fitz pondered that a moment. "True, but I have more weight. It would be harder for him to knock me backwards."

"What if Luna gets him to open the door, and we all charge like a football offensive line?" Ben suggested.

"It might work if we don't trip on each other and all fall on the floor," Fitz said. "Did you say when you'd come?"

Luna blushed again. "No, but I told him you wouldn't have much pep."

Ben laughed. "I love it! When we do this, I expect he'll look out the window to make sure it's Luna and that she's by herself. We'll have to position ourselves so he won't see us."

"Good point," Fitz said. "Luna, if you'll knock and then step just a little toward the window, that will give us more room to charge the door. I hope it's just him and Zee in the room."

Katía snickered.

"What's so funny?" Fitz asked.

"The two of you and the word charging don't exactly fit."

"Ha, ha. We might surprise you," Ben replied.

"Do you think we've waited long enough?" Katía asked.

Fitz looked at his watch. "I have no idea."

They walked down the exterior stairs and got into position outside room 118. Luna cast a worried look their way, then knocked on the door. "Hey, it's me." Nothing happened, so she knocked again.

The door swung open, a hand grabbed Luna's wrist, and she was gone. The door slammed behind her.

"I don't think so," Katía said. She positioned herself in front of the window and kicked with all her might. The glass shattered, and she jumped inside.

As Katía crashed through the window with gun drawn, the door opened and the goon came running out, crashing right into Ben. He tripped and hit the ground. Fitz planted his knee in the middle of the man's back. "That's far enough."

The man tried to get up, but Fitz's weight was too much. Ben rose to one knee and placed the barrel of his gun to the thug's head. "Don't move or it's over."

"You still have those zip ties?" Fitz asked.

"Of course I still have them." Ben pulled the pack out of his coat pocket, and Fitz tied the guy's feet and hands. Then he jumped up to check the room.

Gun at the ready, he peeked around the door. He relaxed when he saw Katía and Luna hugging Zee. As usual, Zee was handcuffed to the bed.

As soon as Fitz stepped into the room, a chill ran down his spine. "Get that guy in here quick!" He helped Ben drag him into the room and closed the door.

"Good thinking. We're behind enemy lines," Ben said.

"Call Chief Arnold and let him know we need help."

Ben pushed the gang member onto the bed and made the call. "This is Ben from earlier at the medical facility. We've located the hostage, but we might be in a jam. We're at Motel Six on Monroe Drive. It appears to be headquarters for Confederate Rising… That's the problem. We've captured one of their own and are holed up in a room with the window broken out… We're in room one eighteen. Get some officers you trust over here."

CHAPTER 54

Fitz pulled the curtain closed over the broken window. "Katía, over there and watch that way." He pointed away from the side of the room to which he had directed her. "I'll watch this way. Ben, see if you can find the key to the cuffs."

"Got it and another gun," Ben said, having already started searching the captive. He handed the gun to Luna. She took the handle with her thumb and index finger.

"I don't know how to use this thing," she said.

"OK, just make sure no one else gets it," Ben replied as he moved to unlock Zee.

Zee rubbed his wrist where the cuffs had been. "I sure am glad to see you guys! I was worried sick after they took Katía away."

"Me, too," Katía said.

"I think you should have a turn with these," Ben said, cuffing the gang member's wrists on top of the zip ties.

Fitz aimed his gun through the slit in the drapes. He watched as a man with the telltale tattoo walked toward the room. His heart pounded in his chest as the man got closer. *I hope he walks on by.*

When he was about five feet from the room, he reached behind his back. "Stop or you're a dead man," Fitz boomed.

The man pulled a gun from the waist of his pants. As soon as Fitz saw it, he fired. The guy fell backward and rolled off the sidewalk and behind a car. The gun was nowhere to be seen.

"Everybody down," Fitz called, taking a knee by the window as he scanned for signs of the injured man. "He's not dead and may try to shoot again." A flicker of hope formed when Fitz heard sirens in the distance.

"Call Chief Arnold back and tell him there's a man with a gun behind the gray Toyota Camry in front of our room," Fitz directed.

"We have another vulture coming," Katía said, bracing herself to fire. "He leaned against the wall, and I can't see him," she whispered.

Fitz readied himself for an attack right at the edge of the window on his side.

"I'm here to help. Is anyone hurt?" a smooth voice called. "The coast is clear. You can come out now."

"No, thanks. We're happy where we are," Fitz called back. He heard a couple of quiet steps. "If you come any closer, you'll regret it."

A shot exploded the wall just over Katía's head. She ducked lower, just peering out the bottom corner of the window. The pause lasted a few seconds. The sound of sirens got closer.

Fitz signaled for Katía to get on the floor. Three shots exploded in rapid succession. The goon stepped past the edge of the window where Fitz crouched, continuing to fire.

Fitz shot him right under the left arm, and he careened into the parking lot, landing in a still heap.

Ben was still on the phone with the chief. "There's another one down in the parking lot… Yeah, we're still OK."

It seemed like three hours had passed before three patrol cars zoomed into the parking lot. Six officers jumped out and secured the area, including relieving the first injured guy of his gun. The other one's gun lay on the sidewalk. Fitz feared he was dead. An ambulance followed just after the patrol cars arrived.

Fitz eyed the officers warily, wondering if any were corrupt. One officer noticed Fitz looking through the gap in the drape. He leveled his gun at Fitz and called, "Gainesville Police. Come out with your hands up."

"Thank God you're here," Katía called, popping up from the floor. "We're coming out."

"I hope these are the good guys." Fitz holstered his gun, opened the door, and put up his hands.

The officer lowered his weapon. "Hey, Fitz. They didn't tell me it was you causing all this trouble."

Fitz could feel his heart rate slowing down at the sight of his old friend. "Hey, Wayne. I expected you to be retired by now."

"It's coming up in five months. I'm counting down each day. Is everyone OK in there?"

"Yeah. A little rattled, but no one is injured. Right folks?" he called over his shoulder.

"Zee might need some checking over," Ben said, helping Zee walk out of the room.

Zee squinted in the sunlight. "I need to find King. I hope he's not dead in my car."

"He's fat and happy, living the good life at my house with Snickers," Ben replied.

"Thanks, but how did he get to your house?"

"It's a long story," Ben chuckled. "Officers, I sure am grateful to you. There's a guy stuck to the bed in there you might be interested in. He could be the ring leader of this bunch."

Fitz watched as they loaded the first man he had shot into the ambulance. A second ambulance pulled up just as they shut the doors. Paramedics jumped out and checked the second man Fitz had shot. Fitz braced himself.

Suddenly, the paramedics jumped into high gear, got the man loaded into the ambulance, and raced off. Relief washed over Fitz, and he exhaled. *At least he's not dead. I don't like killing folks even if they're trying to kill me.*

Fitz noticed people peeking out of doors and windows all over the motel. *That's not surprising. We caused quite a commotion.* He felt the chill in his spine again. It was always a warning. *Some of those folks could be armed.* "Everybody on the sidewalk!"

"What is it, Fitz?" Wayne asked.

"There could be other gang members ready to take target practice."

"Gather up," Wayne called to the other officers. "We have to clear the building. Room to room searches and apprehend anyone with a Confederate flag tattooed on their neck. Let's have two on the first floor and three on the second. I'll stay with these folks."

The officers left, and Fitz listened as they knocked on door after door and announced themselves. *I hope no one gets shot.*

Wayne started taking statements while the other officers searched. Fitz explained how they had found the place through the social media post, located the one who had Zee, and ended up in the room for the shootout.

"If my husband hears about what I said to that creep, I'll just die," Luna groaned. She handed over the gang member's gun.

The officers returned. "We didn't find anyone with the tattoo on their neck, but no one answered at ten of the doors. We wrote down those room numbers," Officer Powell said.

"Good. Let's get these folks out of here and to the police station where it's safe," Wayne said. "I think we have sufficient cause to enter those rooms. Powell, keep an eye out and make sure no one sneaks out."

"Yes, sir," Officer Powell said as he stepped into the parking lot and crouched down behind one of the patrol cars to monitor the rooms.

"That's my car," Ben said, pointing to his Outback.

"Do you promise to go straight to the station so we can finish your statements?" Wayne turned his eyes on Fitz.

"We'll go straight there," Fitz answered, his voice a bit testy.

"Could we hit Burger King on the way? I sure am sick of granola bars," Zee said.

"Two more of you get out there and provide cover. When they're in position, run to your car and get out of here," Wayne ordered.

They hustled to Ben's car, and he raced out of the parking lot. On the way to Burger King, Fitz said, "When this is all over, I'm going to have all of you over for a steak dinner."

"What do you mean, 'Have us over?'" Ben asked.

"We'll have one of the best views in the county," Fitz answered.

CHAPTER 55

Fitz listened to the news on the local radio station as he drove to the grocery store the next day. It was all about the arrests the day before. They had discovered that Dr. Herringer was implanting deep brain stimulators into his victims in an attempt to find a way to treat dementia.

He had bypassed animal experimentation, preferring instead to experiment on people he considered to be expendable: African Americans. He was alleged to have recruited the local members of Confederate Rising to abduct his subjects. Authorities knew of one fatality for which he was alleged to be responsible, but expected to find more since his documentation indicated Katía would have been his eighth victim.

Fitz shuddered when they said that. *That would have been horrible. I'm so glad we found her before they did it.*

As he parked the car, Fitz thought back over yesterday. *King was ecstatic when Zee walked into Ben's house. His tail wagging muscles are probably sore today. I was surprised when Ben invited Katía and Zee to stay the night. He thought it might be scary to stay by themselves. I was even more surprised when Zee took him up on his offer. He said he could get used to sleeping in a bed. This is a good group of folks. I'm glad I've gotten to know them.*

He checked his bank account a second time. *This is going to be a strain, but I want to do it.* He spent a long time choosing the best looking New York strip steaks, got a package of Bar-B-Q bread, then selected two salad packs that included the dressing. At the deli section, he picked out chocolate chip cookies for dessert.

I forgot charcoal. He went back across the store, put a bag into his buggy, then added up the price in his head. *I've got this.* His hands clamped down on the buggy handle anyway.

He arrived at the cul-de-sac by the lake at 4:15pm. Everyone was coming at five. *We should be watching the sun set as we eat. Perfect.*

In the mornings people were often fishing, one guy would launch his kayak, and a jogger would come by. In the evenings, he usually had this spot to himself. He was counting on that for the celebration tonight.

Making the fire ring a little larger, he lit the charcoal. He set up his camp chair and hooked Buffett to his leash. "You need some fresh air, my friend. I apologize for leaving you so much lately."

"Meow."

"You're so understanding."

Looping the leash around the leg of the chair, he sat down. Buffett sniffed around for a bit then hopped into his lap. It had been a nice February day, and the temperature was 51 degrees. *The fire makes this just right.*

Fitz sat up straight and smiled at the sound of a car approaching. It was Ben's Outback.

"Thanks for bringing the plates and silverware, especially the steak knives," Fitz said as Ben got out and leashed up Snickers.

"You're welcome. Thanks for hosting."

Snickers went straight to Buffett, and they sniffed over each other.

"Wow! This is a pretty place," Ben noted.

"It's one of my favorite spots."

The sound of other cars drew Fitz's eyes up the road. Zee's car no longer had its squeal. "I see Zee changed the belt."

"Yeah, I supervised him this morning."

Katía, Zee, and Luna and her husband all arrived at the same time. Katía jumped out and started hugging everyone. Fitz stiffened when she got to him. He slowly wrapped his arms around her and hugged her back. It was his first hug since losing Sharon.

"Hey, everybody, this is Carlos," Luna said, taking her husband's arm. "Carlos, these are the park pals I've been telling you about."

Zee led King over to Snickers and Buffett. They seemed happy to see each other. The sun floated just above the tree line as Fitz put the steaks onto the grill. A murder of crows gabbed nearby.

"We might have company," Fitz said. "The crows are used to people leaving food behind."

"They ain't gettin' my steak. I've been lookin' forward to this all day," Zee said.

"I love crows. They're some of the smartest critters on the planet," Katía added.

Fitz passed around the salad bags then served up the steaks. He placed the bread on the grill, and Katía said, "Do you mind if we have a blessing before we eat?"

Everyone bowed, and she prayed, "God, thank you so much for this food and these wonderful people. Without them, I wouldn't be here today. I'm grateful for their friendship and the way you have brought them into my life. Amen."

When everyone opened their eyes, the sky bathed the earth in a pink glow.

"Wow! This is gorgeous!" Luna said.

Fitz flipped the bread as they took their first bites of steak. The conversation took a serious turn.

"Zee, how did you survive being chained to a bed for so long?" Luna asked.

"It wasn't too hard. I had everything I needed except King and my freedom. I just sat and waited. Then Katía came and kept me company. That was a blessing."

"I can't believe what that guy was doing to people," Carlos said.

"I wonder if it worked. My memory's gettin' shabby. I might be willin' to try it, as long as I wasn't forced," Zee said.

"I guess we'll never know. That doctor is going to be locked up for a long time. They're holding him without bail." Katía added.

As everyone finished up their steaks, Fitz offered the cookies for dessert.

"You're quite the host," Ben chuckled.

The light slipped away, and the air chilled. "I guess it's time to get going," Luna said. "We'll have to do this again. I'd love to have you guys over."

"That would be great," Ben agreed. "Maybe we could take turns."

"We'll have to make some plans at the park in the morning. Will everyone be there?" Katía asked.

"I will," Ben said.

"It seems like a long time since we've met at the park," Fitz added.

"Amen to that," Katía said.

The group started moving to their cars, slowly as if they didn't really want to part.

"You want to come back to the house?" Ben asked Zee.

"Nah, I think it's time I got back to my real life. Thank you, though. Besides, how can you leave this beautiful place?"

Fitz and Zee returned to their chairs by the dwindling fire. Zee pulled a napkin from his pocket, unfolded it, and offered King and Buffett three bites of steak each. "I reckon it's going to get cold tonight."

"Feels like it," Fitz answered. "You want to stay here?"

"I thought I would, if that's OK with you, of course."

"It'll be nice to have the company." Those were words Fitz never dreamed he would say.

They pulled their chairs closer to the charcoal to take advantage of the last embers glowing in the dark. *I think I'm tired of being alone.*

ACKNOWLEDGMENTS

Writing a book takes a village! I am grateful to B. J. Myers-Bradley, Clara Bella Rose, and Yvette Summerour for reading through the manuscript and providing feedback that made this a better book. I'm endebted to Cheshire Adams, Community Coordinator for Good News at Noon, Armando Guillen, and Jonathan Humphrey for helping me to understand the lifestyles of residentially challenged folks. As always, I'm indebted to Merilyn Guerry for her amazing editorial skills.

I am also grateful for the artistic skills of Getcovers for the cover design and Becky Franks for the author photo.

Most importantly, I am grateful to you for investing your time in reading **The Hidden Scalpel**. It would be quite helpful if you would take a moment to leave a review or rating on the site from which you purchased the book.

COMING SOON! BOOK 2 IN THE PARK PALS SERIES: THE MISSING PILL
Watch for it in early 2025!

Other books by Dwain Cassady:
The Dark Wings Trilogy:
Dark Wings Rising, Dark Wings Daring, and Dark Wings Soaring.

www.ingramcontent.com/pod-product-compliance
Lightning Source LLC
Chambersburg PA
CBHW061121310726
48974CB00002B/628